WEREWOLVES AND WENDIGO

WEREWOLVES AND WENDIGO

PENNY AND BOOTS™ BOOK TWO

AMY HOPKINS

MICHAEL ANDERLE

DISRUPTIVE IMAGINATION

LMBPN Publishing
PMB 196, 2540 South Maryland Pkwy
Las Vegas, NV 89109

First US edition, November 2019
eBook ISBN: 978-1-64202-535-4
Print ISBN: 978-1-64202-536-1

WEREWOLVES AND WENDIGO TEAM

Thanks to our Beta Readers:
Mary Morris, Larry Omans, Kelly O'Donnell, Nicole
Emens, Michael Baumann

Thanks to the JIT Readers

Angel LaVey
Jackey Hankard-Brodie
Dave Hicks
Misty Roa
Deb Mader
Jeff Eaton
Paul Westman

If I've missed anyone, please let me know!

Editor
SkyHunter Editing Team

I was going to dedicate this book to my cat. Then I remembered I don't have one.

— Amy

To Family, Friends and
Those Who Love
to Read.
May We All Enjoy Grace
to Live the Life We Are
Called.

— Michael

"Penny? What is *that*?" Amelia pointed at the orange and brown crocheted throw in Penny's hands. "Tell me you didn't fly to the other side of the world just to bring it back?"

"Of course not." Penny threw the blanket at her. "I flew across the world to bring it back and give it to you!"

Amelia squealed, hurling the dusty blanket back at Penny. "No! It's probably infested with bed bugs." She watched as Boots haughtily took the edge of the blanket between her fangs and pulled it into her sleeping basket. "Or worse, Bunyips." Her eyes narrowed. "Did you *really* see one while you were back home?"

Penny grinned. "I didn't just see it. I chased the damn thing through two paddocks and a stream. I almost caught it, too!"

Amelia snorted. "*Almost* isn't good enough, girl. I bet you were holding back!"

"What if I was?" Penny taunted. "It's not like I had a chopper on call to pick the thing up."

"Fair enough." Amelia frowned. "So, what elective track did you choose for this semester?"

Penny's paperwork hadn't been submitted until the last minute. The dean had sent a frantic email while Penny was away, asking her to choose a career track within the Mythological Resurgence course immediately so that scheduling could be worked out. "Field, of course. You're doing it too, right?"

Amelia shook her head. "Me, trekking through muddy forests and oozing swamps to chase down Chupacabras? No thanks. I picked Media since it covers a lot of political stuff which I can use if I ever want to go mainstream with the qualifications."

"Oh." Penny's exuberance at being back in America and back at the academy dropped a couple of notches. She had assumed she would be in classes with her best friend again. "Well, I guess it's only two classes we have apart. What did Red pick?"

The Irishman had been dithering between Field Training and Forensics, last she'd heard. Amelia's texts and emails had been frequent over the two weeks Penny had been absent, but somehow contained little information.

Well, unless you counted the long list of parties and events she'd been to, who she had seen there, and which celebrities she'd spotted over the winter break.

"He went with Forensics." Amelia gave her a sly smile. "You're not going to ask about Cisco?"

"What? Of course, I am." Penny turned away to hide the pink in her cheeks. "What did he choose?"

"Don't even pretend you weren't Skyping him daily," Amelia said. "He ran off the same time every morning with that doe-eyed look on his face! I bet you know exactly what track he chose—and what he had for breakfast every day, and who he spoke to, and everything else he did while you were gone."

Penny cringed. "That obvious, huh?"

Amelia nodded. "At least he'll be in Field Training with you. Ugh, I couldn't even imagine being stuck in a class with Clive and Jason otherwise."

"No Corey?" Penny asked with relief.

Amelia shook her head, eyes sparkling. "Not according to the gossip." She lowered her voice to a whisper. "He got kicked out. He failed *two* classes, then went batshit at Professor Madera when she wouldn't change his grade. They tossed him for poor conduct."

"What?" Penny screeched with glee. "He went off on Madera? How did he think she'd let *that* slide?" Shaking her head, she dumped the last few items out of her duffel bag.

She set a ballerina figurine beside her bed next to a photo of her parents. It had been a gift from her nan—too valuable to risk for a short trip, too sentimental to leave behind if she was staying.

"Gee, Penny, it almost looks like you're moving in for real this time." Amelia flopped down on her bed and eyed Penny's once-bare side table. "You *are*, aren't you?"

"I am." Penny set her hands on her hips and nodded once, satisfied with the tiny arrangement. "Now I just have to figure out how to afford it."

Dinner that evening was at seven, sharp, according to the email Penny had received two days prior. She had missed the Academy's first welcome dinner five months ago, so she had made sure she'd be back in time to attend this one.

When she entered the dining hall, she immediately wished she'd dressed up a little for it. The number of students had doubled thanks to the mid-year intake, and Penny counted a dozen teachers, up from the four she had met the previous year. With them, Special Agent Crenel, the appointed Academy liaison and his wife, Dean March.

It still blew Penny's mind to know the bristly agent and the immaculate dean were married. *Although it does explain a lot*, Penny had to admit. For starters, why Crenel was so damn involved with the Academy to start with. Not to mention how hard he had worked to get the Academy affiliated with the Bureau.

Penny took a seat at the end of a long table, glad to see Cisco and Red already there. Cisco quickly jumped up as she approached and pulled a chair out for her.

"Glad to see you back," he said with a grin. "How was the trip?"

"Good." Penny awkwardly sat, trying not to step on his toes as he pushed the chair back in under her.

"Would you two just sleep together already?" Red asked in a bored tone, ruined by a chuckle. "Poor Cisco's been pining away for you, Penny. Two weeks without his— Ow!" He rubbed the bicep Cisco had punched and quickly changed topics. "How was your New Year?"

"Amazing," Penny gushed, her mind flying back to the night in the hotel overlooking the Brisbane River. They'd been drinking champagne on the balcony, the perfect spot to watch the midnight fireworks. "Mum and Dad were pretty devastated when I told them I was coming back. It was a nice way to say goodbye."

"Speaking of goodbye, how far away is my wee girl?" Red glanced at the empty doorway.

"Just putting the last touches of makeup on," Penny reassured him. "She'll be here soon."

The clink of metal on glass rang out, and Dean March stood and cleared her throat. "Attention. Attention, students! No, Clive, that won't be necessary…"

She was too late. Clive's holler of, "Be quiet!" rang across the hall loudly.

Dean March gave a patient sigh. "Thank you. That's quite enough, Clive." She lifted her head and addressed the room. "Thank you, students. Welcome to the March-Blaisey Academy of Myth and Legend. Most of you are returning from last semester. I hope you'll join me in wishing the new students all the best as they begin their courses tomorrow morning."

A limp cheer went up from a few students, and the dean waited until it died down before proceeding. "Of course, you will all know by now about the changes this semester. Though we retain a level of independence, the March-Blaisey Academy is no longer a private institute. Special Agent Stuart Crenel is here to explain what that means."

A smatter of applause went around the room as the dean sat and the agent stood. Crenel pulled out a crumpled bit of paper and squinted at it. "That's not it," he muttered.

Dean March smoothly passed him a crisply folded sheet, and he took it with a raised eyebrow. "I made a copy," she explained.

"You did? Of course, you did. Thanks." Agent Crenel cleared his throat. "The March-Blaisey Academy of Myth and Legend is now the second training institute to be officially recognized by the Federal Bureau of Investigation. The FBI has worked with the Academy to ensure the curriculum will not only turn out the best-equipped students to assist in Mythological Threat Management, but your qualifications will be of specific value to the bureau."

He paused, running his eyes over the watching students. "As an entity now under the umbrella of the FBI, you will be expected to comport yourselves with this in mind. There will be instances in which your skills will be called upon, even before you graduate. Unfortunately, the situation out there isn't willing to sit back and wait until school's out.

Crenel's face was serious. "You can and will be called upon to assist the FBI during your time at the Academy. The accomplishments you make in the field will be reflected in your final grades. In addition, the missions you are given will impact the people outside. You will be doing your part to ensure America is, and always remains, the land of the free."

He sat down quickly and downed the glass of wine by his plate, then wiped his face with his napkin.

Watching Dean March's long-suffering expression, Penny wondered how she'd ever thought the two were anything *but* husband and wife.

Dean March stood again. "Now, those of you returning this year will see some new faces. I'd like to introduce our faculty, new and old. Professor Glass will replace Professor

Jones, who was relieved of his position after endangering the life of a student."

A man stood, ignoring the titter of surprise that ran around the new students.

Penny knew the story of her Defense exam had already been passed around by everyone who'd been there for the first semester. She examined this new professor carefully, wondering if he'd been told which student was responsible for Jones' termination.

Glass was younger than Jones, with shaggy hair and the slightest bristle of beard. Where Jones was large framed and obviously strong, Glass was small and wiry. Still, he watched the room with intelligent eyes. When he stood, his couple of steps forward were awkward and shuffling. He nodded and maneuvered back to his chair, bending down to adjust one leg after he sat.

Prosthetic? Penny wondered.

"Professor Anand will be taking Cross-Cultural Mythology this year. She will also be adding Indian Mythology and Cyber-Mythology to the curriculum next year."

Anand stood, giving the students a shallow bow as she watched them over silver-rimmed glasses.

She immediately reminded Penny of Professor Madera. The two were of a similar age, and each had a no-nonsense look about them.

Penny noted and immediately forgot about the next two professors, both taking classes for the electives she had decided against.

Professor Quaid's introduction, though, snapped her back to attention.

"Most of you here know Agent Crenel personally," March was saying. "Well, this is the man who taught him."

The grizzled agent-turned-professor scowled, crossing his arms as he endured the curious looks of the fifty students. He stood, jerked a nod at them, then sat down with the same irritation his former protégé had shown earlier.

March informed the students that one of the new professors was absent. Professor Blaisey would arrive in time for his first class on Friday.

"You will note that Professor Blaisey shares his last name with the Academy itself." Dean March gave a small smile. "He is, in fact, the financial backer of this fine institution. I hope you will give him all the respect that deserves, despite his…unorthodox teaching methods."

March quickly introduced Professor McClure, a ridiculously handsome psychology professor and Professor Smith, the media studies teacher. Once done, she sat and gestured for the students to talk among themselves.

"Wow. So many people," Penny said. She glanced over the hubbub to see the doors crack open as Amelia slipped through.

Her friend hurried over to their table, where Penny had saved her a seat. "I guess the mid-year intake was a success," Amelia said. She craned her neck to look at the head table. "Wow. Who's the hottie? *Please* tell me I've got him for a class."

Red sighed. "Are you telling me I have to be jealous of the bloody psychology professor now? It was bad enough when you spent three weeks yabbering about how cute that magic party guy was."

"God," Amelia corrected him. "Bacchus wasn't a *guy*, he was a god. And a really hot one, too." She leaned over to peck Red on the cheek. "None of them can hold a candle to you, my dear, but I have to have *something* nice to look at when you're not around."

Red grumbled good-naturally, then looked up with glee when a platter of hot meat appeared at the table, courtesy of Cook.

The old woman had a suspiciously warm glow to her face. "You'll like today's dinner," she said with a wink. "I had a bit of help with it, you see." She gestured to a man carrying past a tray of drinks, headed toward the head table.

"Oh, strike me down. It's him, isn't it?" Red groaned and sank into his seat.

It certainly looks like Bacchus, Penny realized. *But what the hell is he doing here?*

"How in the world did you wrangle a god to help you in the kitchen?" Cisco asked.

Cook giggled. "Not me, love. Dean March organized it, something about an alliance of some sort. I wasn't really listening, to be honest." She leaned forward conspiratorially. "I was too busy watching him. He's very handsome, he is!" She urged the students to "eat up so you don't all waste away," then left to continue serving food.

"I *really* hate that guy," Red muttered.

Amelia nudged him. "Don't be ridiculous. He was very polite when we met him. He hasn't done anything to you!"

Red threw his hands up in defeat. "Aye, I'll just go and make best friends with the handsome god my girlfriend is drooling over. Why not?"

He shoved himself up from the table and, ignoring Amelia's hissed protests, strode over to intercept Bacchus on his way back to the kitchen.

The god—*he really is handsome*, Penny thought— listened to Red and nodded sagely.

When Red returned, it was with his new friend in tow. "There you go," Red said with a smirk. "Bacchus himself. Scoot over, Penny, and I'll grab him a chair."

Penny did so with an internal groan. She still hadn't quite forgiven Bacchus for promising them all the secrets of the Mythers, then making them promptly forget everything he had revealed.

"Greetings, old friends." Bacchus smiled and took the chair Red offered him. "It is good to see you again." He drew a plate out of nowhere and began to pile on food. A quick hand wave, and he had a glass of deep-red wine.

"One for us?" Amelia asked.

Bacchus laughed. "Apologies, Amelia. Your representative instructed me that only the higher ranks of your organization may imbibe tonight." He gestured to the head table and the professors.

Curiosity burned away Penny's frustration with him. "Maybe next time." She motioned to the platter of meat. "I hear you're to thank for the food?"

Bacchus shook his head. "Your chef is a delightfully talented woman. I merely assisted in tonight's preparations."

"And why is that?" Penny asked. She casually slid some beef onto her plate and drizzled it with gravy but didn't eat any.

"Politics," Bacchus said, watching her. "My people are

aware of what Jessica March is attempting here. We thought it best if we showed we are with her, not against her."

"And what exactly is she attempting?" Cisco asked, stuffing a hot roll in his mouth before he'd quite finished speaking.

"Why, assembling an army, of course!" Bacchus chuckled. "An army of young, virile warriors, trained to protect the populace from the demons summoned forth from the Veil."

"And you want to...what, help?" Penny couldn't keep the skepticism from her voice. "Weren't you summoned forth from the Veil?"

"I want to ensure the demons are not confused with the benevolent gods." He placed his hand on hers and looked deep into Penny's eyes. "Many of my kind have come here simply by chance. All we wish is for the right to exist. We mean no harm, and we have caused no hurt." His grip tightened. "Others? Their motives are far more nefarious."

He released Penny's hand and ran his eyes over Amelia, Cisco, and Red. "We hope for an alliance that will benefit both your people and mine. Tonight is the beginning of such a relationship. Let us drink to the occasion."

Penny glanced at her empty cup, meaning to remind him that they weren't able to drink. To her surprise, it was filled with cloudy amber liquid.

"Fermented ginger. I may not agree with your laws about alcohol, but I abide by them. This is legal even for the youngest among you," Bacchus explained. He leaned down so his lips were by her ear. "You may eat and drink, child. Nothing that happens tonight will be lost in your memory."

Penny took a wary sip of the ginger drink. It fizzed gently, the hot tang warming her tongue. "It's nice," she said. "Really nice."

"Surely, you expected no less?" Bacchus grinned and stood. "Alas, I must return to my duties. There is a poor child over there feeling quite lonely and homesick. As the god of festivities, I cannot let that stand." He bowed deeply and sauntered away.

Penny watched him go. "He's crazy," she said. "But I want to know more about this alliance."

"I wish I could do that." Amelia pouted at her cup, already empty. She waved her hand over it, using the same gesture the god had. Nothing happened.

"Have mine." Red pushed his glass to her. "I've had enough ginger jokes in my life to turn me off the stuff for good. That, and carrots." He shuddered in disgust.

"Cisco, do you think your Mom can shed any light on Bacchus's plans?" Penny waited for him to swallow the mouthful of food he was chewing.

He shrugged. "Probably not. This new deal with the feds means half of what she knows is classified."

"What about the other half?" Amelia asked.

He grimaced. "It's class stuff, which means it's boring."

CHAPTER TWO

"Ready?" Professor Glass waited for Penny and Mara to drop into defensive stances before quickly walking over. "No! Mara, that stance is terrible. Put your feet like this." He kicked Mara's feet into the correct position with an awkward movement.

Penny quickly checked her own feet, relieved to see they matched her opponent's.

"Begin!" Glass stepped back to watch the two students spar, his arms folded across his chest.

Mara adjusted her weight and Penny took a quick step back, raising her arms to a blocking position.

When Mara's shoulders twisted, Penny ducked under the fist that followed.

Penny stepped to the side and jabbed a quick punch at Mara's ribs, thrusting from her hip. Her opponent was slower, but Mara took the blow without flinching.

Penny waited for Mara to move again. She caught the snap kick, throwing Mara's foot back to tip her off balance. A moment later, Mara was on the floor, flat on her back.

"You're not fast, but damn, you can take a punch." Penny leaned in, one hand outstretched to help her opponent up.

Mara smirked, and instead of taking her hand, she shoved a foot at Penny's hip.

Penny curled over to take the blow, but Mara's foot hooked her ankle, and suddenly, Penny was the one on the floor with Mara standing over her.

"Cheap shot," Penny grumbled. She rolled to dodge a sharp heel-kick to the head and scrambled back across the floor, putting a distance of several feet between them.

Mara crouched low, grinning. "No, *you* let your guard down. Who has the upper hand now?"

"Fair point." Penny twisted away from Mara's charge, coming to her feet before she flipped the other girl onto her back.

Penny used her leg to pin the other girl down. "Won't let it happen again." She grabbed an arm and yanked it around.

"Ahh!" Mara withstood the twisted arm with grace for about three seconds. Then, she slapped the floor. "Okay, okay! I give up!"

Glass limped over, looking down at the defeated student. "You're both too damn cocky. Penny should have had that round in the first few moves. Mara, you had her at a disadvantage, and you still lost. You both let your confidence get the better of you."

He waited for Mara to stand and brush herself off before turning back to the rest of the watching class. "The moment you think you have won is the moment you are most likely to lose. It's when you take your eyes off your opponent, when you relax and let your guard down." He turned back to Mara. "It's when your focus turns to celebrating your win instead of securing it."

"It's just a class," Mara muttered. "Lighten up, Prof."

Glass stepped up to her, his body inches away. He slowly raised his hand, holding it palm-out. The hand snapped back and punched forward, stopping just short of Mara's face.

Her eyes widened.

"The creatures we are dealing with are ruthless. Do you think they won't target you here? Or do you realize that training to destroy them might *make* you a target?" Glass shook his head. "You're an idiot if you think this place is impenetrable. The defenses of the Academy are pathetic. A bunch of old teachers, washed up agents, and some untrained students. And our enemy? They're not as stupid as you are."

Ignoring the disgruntled protests of his students, Glass called up the next duo for sparring. "Cisco. Clive. You're up."

Penny stepped away from the foam mat, her attention on Glass's words. *Enemy? Not all the Mythers are malicious.*

She reassured herself that it was just—could *only* be—a figure of speech. Dean March had been adamant that part of the duties of the Academy was to foster understanding between humans and Mythers. Otherwise, why would Bacchus be here?

Clive and Cisco sprang into action at the professor's call. Where Mara and Penny had waited, assessing each other's moves, the two boys sparred ruthlessly without pause.

Clive threw a punch, Cisco ducked and struck out with a foot. Clive spun away to dodge and backhanded Cisco in the kidneys.

"That's gotta hurt," Red groaned.

Penny winced in sympathy as Cisco's fist shot toward Clive's stomach. Clive doubled over but Cisco hobbled back, sucking in a pained breath.

"Stop!" Glass yelled. "Have you listened to a damn thing I've said? You back off like that, and your enemy will rip you to pieces before you can blink." He gestured for the boys to leave the mat. "Class dismissed. I'll come up with something for you to do next lesson that won't involve pissing about like a bunch of women."

Amelia snorted, and Penny raised an eyebrow. Rather than respond, Glass turned his back and walked out.

"Bunch of women?" Amelia seethed. "I could kick his ass in a hot minute."

"Well, yeah." Penny went to get her bag beside the door. "I mean, he's only got one leg. It can't be that hard."

"Are you kidding?" Cisco grabbed the backpack and tossed it to her. "That thing is made of cast iron. One good hit and you'd be out cold."

"How do you even *know* that?" Penny demanded. In retrospect, it was believable. Glass's limp made him move less smoothly than a prosthetic would account for, like he was lugging a heavy weight with his missing leg.

For a man who otherwise moved with eerie grace, it had made Penny wonder.

Cisco smirked. "Wouldn't you like to know?"

Penny smiled sweetly. "Cisco, mate. This is the second time I've had to bail you out mid-class due to a lack of stationery. Next time, I'll give you a very special notebook, one with a great big dick drawn on the cover."

Cisco's jaw dropped, and he stared for a moment, stunned. Then, realizing he was on the losing side, he groaned. "Okay! Fine. I would have told you eventually. He's got *three* of the damn things. March had to lug the case upstairs for him."

"He made *Dean March* carry his bags?" Penny's hand covered her mouth. The dean was kind and cared deeply for her students, but she also held strictly to the rules of decorum. Crossing her was unheard of.

Cisco nodded. "Mom saw the whole thing. A real dick, right?"

"Aye, Glass is a big, floppy, dangling dick of epic proportions. One that's impressive for its size and its uselessness." Red finished speaking the barest moment after the training room door swung open and Glass stepped back inside.

The Irishman's eyes grew wide with fear.

"Mister O'Donaghue, despite your apparently exhaustive familiarity with a wide range of penile presentations, I trust you will keep your opinion to yourself from now on." Glass's voice was like his name—hard and brittle.

The professor walked over to the small corner desk, iron leg thumping loudly on the floorboards, and snatched up a stack of papers before turning back to address the class. "You don't need to like me. After all, I don't like any of you. I am, however, going to teach you not to die. And you're going to learn it whether you like dick or not."

He turned and walked out of the room, slamming the door behind him.

"I'm so dead," Red whispered, his face gray. "So, *so* dead."

Penny clapped him on the arm. "All good, mate. You took one for the team. When you die, we'll make sure we fill your coffin with whiskey."

Cisco's face lit up. "Speaking of whiskey, we've got the afternoon off. You wanna hit a bar or something?"

Amelia clicked her tongue. "You might have the afternoon off, but I don't. I've got Psych at midday."

Cisco turned to Red, who shrugged. "I have Research Methodology at three."

Penny winced when Cisco turned desperate eyes on her. "Sorry, Cisco. I managed to line up a job interview for this afternoon."

"What?" Amelia grabbed her arm. "You only got back twenty-four hours ago. How the hell did you manage that?"

Penny laughed. "I was in Australia, not the Middle Ages. I applied online and told them when I'd be back for an interview."

"Oh." Seemingly disappointed there wasn't some strange, magical explanation, Amelia let her hand fall away. "Well, I have to go and feed my hungry face before class."

"I'll come with you," Red quickly said.

Cisco raised his hand and went to say something, but Red looked over his shoulder and shook his head, drawing a hand across his throat.

"Oh." Cisco sighed. "Guess they want to be alone."

"As long as they wash the towels after," Penny shrugged.

"Dining hall?" Cisco held the classroom door open for Penny.

She checked her watch and shook her head. "I really have to go. Maybe after? We can celebrate the success of my amazing charm and impeccable credentials have brought me in landing a job."

Cisco grinned. "You're on!"

CHAPTER THREE

Penny arched to stretch her aching back. The thin plastic chair in the waiting room had been bad enough, but the equally cheap metal version she was sitting on now was, if possible, even harder and more uncomfortable.

"Miss Hingston, what specific skill set do you believe you can offer Good White's on a long term basis if you begin your career here?" Gervais, the greasy-haired manager, stared at Penny's resume with dead eyes, his voice flat and emotionless.

"Uhh..." Penny's mind raced. The advertised job had been for a delivery dock laborer. What the hell kind of experience did one need to shove boxed washing machines around a department store? "I'm fast, reliable, and hard-working."

"You say you're reliable, Miss Hingston, but my records show your application history here. You refused the first interview and requested a later date. Does that sound reliable to you?"

"I was out of the country when I applied." Penny frowned. She knew she'd written that on the request for rescheduling. "I only got back yesterday."

"Out of the country. Hmmm." Gervais stared at the resume again, his eyes fixed on a spot in the middle. "You couldn't have simply returned early? This is a big store, Miss Hingston, and we have schedules to maintain. We can't drop everything to cater to the whim of one employee."

"The ticket cost over a grand," Penny said. He wasn't serious. Was he? "They didn't allow for reschedules, and besides, it's a seventeen-hour flight. I only had fourteen hours' notice for the first interview."

"Hmmm." Gervais's face showed his disapproval. "Taking an earlier flight would have been an excellent sign of reliability and flexibility. Those are what make a good employee."

"That wasn't physically possible," Penny insisted. "An earlier flight still would have gotten me here late for the interview. I said in my application that I wasn't back until—"

"Miss Hingston, making demands of an employer before you've even got the job is not the sign of a good employee."

"Do you even know where Australia is?" Penny's mouth clicked shut, too late to stop the snarky comment from escaping.

"Miss Hingston, I don't think you're going to be a good fit for this organization." Gervais steepled his fingers, looking down his nose at Penny. "We at Good White's pride ourselves on exemplary customer service. Our employees always endeavor to go the extra mile. If you can't do that for an interview, I really don't think a lifetime career here would be in the best interests of this company."

"Lifetime employment?" Penny couldn't keep the sarcasm from her voice. "You're offering three dollars an hour below minimum wage, no benefits, and when I walked in here, the greeter out front told me I'd better be willing to sacrifice my soul to the devil if I ever needed a sick day, all while being nickel and dimed for bathroom breaks and stationary use." She stood, grabbing her handbag off the floor. "You can take your lifetime career and shove it, mate."

Gervais didn't react, he just continued to stare at Penny's application.

Penny was glad she'd used a post box address on the application. *Creepy little motherfucker.* She marched out of the interview and grabbed her phone out of her pocket.

"Hey, Penny! You done?" Cisco's cheerful greeting just rankled her more.

"It was a shit show, but at least I dodged a bullet. Still up for a drink?" Penny crossed her fingers as she waited for his reply. She needed a strong drink to wash Gervais's dead-eyed stare away.

"Sure. We can go to Paddy's?" Cisco suggested.

"Paddy's?" Penny bit her lip. "Are you sure we aren't blacklisted there?"

"I walked past on my way to grab some Mexican the other night. Paddy saw me and dragged me in. He wasn't kidding, Penny. I think he might actually own the place."

Penny chuckled. "Okay, as long as we're not going to

get arrested for what we did on our last visit. I'm on my way."

Just as Penny ended the call, a cab rounded the corner. She hailed it and, ten minutes later, she arrived at Paddy's Irish Bar.

Farewelling the driver, Penny stepped out of the cab and headed for the door.

The bar was buzzing despite the early hour. Several of the patio tables were already taken, and three patrons filed out of the door as Penny approached.

She stepped back and waited for them to pass.

"Ahh, the beautiful Penny." A finger touched her chin, tipping her head up to meet Bacchus's gold-flecked eyes. "What a coincidence. Are you well?"

"I'm fine." Penny pulled back, the unplanned meeting and unasked-for physical contact giving her a serious case of the heebie-jeebies.

Bacchus held her gaze for a moment longer. "You're not. You have some seriously depressing mojo attached to you. Who have you been hanging around, Sophrosyne?"

"Just some deadbeat department store manager," Penny hurriedly explained. Then, "Wait. There's another Greek god in Portland?"

Bacchus laughed. "Just an expression of speech, my dear. Poor old Soph is unlikely to appear any time soon. Her gifts are less appreciated by this society than mine."

Penny nodded, hesitant to admit she had no idea who Sophrosyne even was. *I'll look it up later*, she decided. *And maybe the rest of his friends, too.* "Catch you later, Bacchus." She pointedly turned away from him and entered Paddy's.

The atmosphere inside the bar was different during the

day. The yeasty aroma of beer mingled with rich coffee and hot food.

Penny's stomach growled. She couldn't see Cisco anywhere.

The bartender had given her no more than a bored glance, settling any last fears over her previous visit. She chose a small corner table and sat, burying herself in the menu while she waited.

"Lassie! Ye came back for a wee visit!" Paddy hopped onto the chair across from Penny, grinning. "And what fine occasion might this be, eh? Are we stakin' out a group of evildoers? Huntin' a larderbeast?"

His eagerness lifted Penny's mood immediately. "No, Paddy," she laughed. "I'm here to meet Cisco for a drink, that's all." She leaned down and lowered her voice. "It is safe for me to be here, right? I mean, after what we did last time—"

"Don't worry yerself, dear. Paddy told ye, I own this place. Well, in a manner." He waved away Penny's attempt to question that little bit of information. "Regardless, Old Paddy knows it was a matter of national security, what ye did. He said he won't ban ye from the bar." Paddy wagged a finger. "But it might be a good idea if ye refrained from doin' it again, lass."

"*Old* Paddy?" The leprechaun had used the name as if speaking about someone else.

"Aye!" Paddy thumped his chest. "I'm *the* Paddy. Old Paddy and Old Paddy, they're the ones who do all the business stuff. They bought the bar from Paddy Last, who had it from Paddy Previous, ye see?"

Penny's eyes narrowed suspiciously. "That's... a stretch."

She snatched her phone out and pulled up the search engine.

Before she could tap in a query, Cisco sauntered over.

"Penny, you beat me here!" He snatched a chair from a nearby table and wedged it in next to Paddy's, straddling it backward. "Was I late?"

"Oh, lad!" Paddy looked horrified. "A gentleman should *never* be late for a date!"

"What?" Cisco's face reddened. "It's not a…I mean, is it?" He looked to Penny for confirmation.

Penny couldn't resist teasing him. "I don't know, Cisco. Do you want it to be?"

"I…uhh…this feels like a trap." He looked at Paddy. "Is this a trap?"

Paddy leaned up and whispered in his ear. Cisco went from pink to a deep shade of beetroot. "I'm not saying that!" He hissed angrily. "She'd skin me alive!"

"Well, if ye won't take advice from a leprechaun, yer on yer own." Paddy hopped off the chair and left, stopping at a nearby table to harass a stunning young woman.

"What did he say?" Penny asked, curiosity biting her.

Cisco shook his head, mute.

"Go on." Penny grinned. "If you tell me, I'll buy you a drink." Still, he was mute. "Two drinks?" Her smile had begun to fall away as she wondered what on earth Paddy might have said. "Fine. No drinks, and I'll ask Paddy himself." She glanced over to the leprechaun, still chatting up the girl at a table for one.

"Dammit." Cisco hid his head in his hands. "He said all I had to do was offer to 'put a dozen strong babies in you by the end of the night.'"

"A dozen?" Penny squeaked. She reflexively crossed her legs. "You were right. I would have skinned you alive."

"See?" Cisco huffed. "Why aren't you getting mad at the tiny, green drunk? It didn't come out of *my* mouth."

"It did so, you just repeated it!" Penny let him gape in disbelief a moment before dissolving into giggles. "Oh, Cisco. You're such an easy catch. I was just having you on."

Cisco scowled but was quickly pacified by the offer of a drink.

Penny ordered two glasses of Clydes at the bar. Although whiskey wasn't her usual drink, it seemed wrong not to have it at an Irish bar.

When she returned, Paddy had returned to the table. "I only got two," she warned.

Paddy raised an almost full glass. "It's fine, lass. I got meself a drink already."

Penny slipped back into her seat and took a sip, holding the amber fire in her mouth a moment before swallowing. "Wowser. It really grows on you, doesn't it?" She raised her glass to clink it against Cisco's.

"To a new semester," he toasted. "And long friendships."

"Did I miss much while I was gone?" Penny asked. "Any big adventures you forgot to tell me about?"

They'd spoken almost daily while she was away, so Penny was surprised when Cisco pursed his lips, then nodded.

"Just before you got back, actually. Not an adventure, but Mr. March came in for a briefing. I was in March's office when he showed up, and he let me listen in."

"You mean Agent Crenel?" Penny's shoulders tightened.

"What was it?" An FBI briefing could be nothing, just more information on the academy merger. Or…

"They couldn't find Tobias," Cisco said quietly. The cult leader had run during the chaos at the Willamette River. "He's gone, totally off-grid. Not only that, some of the group members disappeared with him."

Penny jolted upright. "What? They just vanished? You don't think the Kraken…"

Cisco shook his head. "All the footage said they got away clean."

"But the spell was broken!" Penny realized she'd raised her voice and quickly lowered it again. "They weren't under his control anymore."

"Aye, ye broke the spell," Paddy interjected.

Cisco shrugged. "Maybe they followed him voluntarily."

The idea made Penny sick to her stomach. "How could they? He was a creep."

"*Absolute* creep." Paddy threw back the last of his drink.

"How could a bunch of emo teens follow a guy who promised them chaos and magic?" Cisco asked dryly.

"Chaos is a big draw," Paddy agreed. Realizing his two drinking partners were staring, he shrugged. "I don't have a damn clue what yer talkin' about. I just don't want to drink alone."

"What happened to your friend?" Penny asked. She looked around, but the pretty girl was gone.

"She was only here to see Bacchus," Paddy admitted. "Once I told her he'd already left, she decided wee Paddy wasn't so fun to talk to after all." He stared into his empty cup morosely, then yelled, "*Lizbet*! Another drink!"

"I'm not your slave, little man." The girl at the bar

continued to polish it, rolling her eyes when she caught Penny looking. "Get it yourself."

Grumbling, Paddy made his way off his chair and tottered toward the bar.

"Do you think Tobias is still around?" Penny asked. The idea of Tobias still lurking in Portland chilled her bones.

Cisco drew closer. "Crenel can't say for sure, but there are rumors of a new coven out by the coast. Not the type they usually get, bonfires and orgies. This group is sneaking around putting up shrines to old gods and local myths."

"Damn." Penny shivered and downed the rest of her drink. Seeing Paddy was still at the bar, she gave a quick whistle between her teeth, and when the leprechaun looked, she held up her empty glass.

"Two!" Cisco called.

"I can hear him muttering from here." Penny giggled.

Still, Paddy returned with a glass of whiskey for each of them.

Penny raised her glass to him. "Thanks, little green man."

"Don't be getting' smart, lass." Paddy winked. "Paddy may be short, but he's not little."

Penny groaned, trying to banish the image of a naked leprechaun from her mind. "I'm gonna pretend I didn't hear that."

"Are ye hard of hearin', lass?" Paddy climbed onto the table and cupped his hands around his mouth. "WEE PADDY IS HUNG LIKE A HORSE, LASS."

"Paddy!" Cisco yanked the leprechaun back down to his seat. "Can't take you anywhere."

"Ye didn't *take* me anywhere," Paddy said smugly. "Ye came to Paddy."

"And don't we regret it." Penny grabbed the menu off the table. "Look, as long as we're here, I'm starving. Are we gonna order some lunch, or what?"

CHAPTER FOUR

"Wakey wakey, girl with snakey."

Penny felt a tug on her toe. "Go away," she groaned.

Amelia persisted, yanking Penny's blanket off and sending a rush of freezing air over her bare skin. "Seriously! You said you had to get up early today. You made me promise not to let you sleep in!"

"I was an idiot!" Penny snapped. "And a liar. I don't need to get up early. Not this early, anyway." She tried to grab her blanket, but Amelia held it just out of her reach.

Amelia tried a different tack. "Boots is hungry."

"Boots can go months without food." Penny made to grab the blanket again, but Boots reared and hissed. "Well, you *can!*"

Clearly outnumbered, Penny surrendered. She rolled out of bed and quickly dressed, hugging her arms to herself until the fabric of her coat warmed against her skin.

"You're definitely up?" Amelia asked warily.

"Yes. Thank you." Penny knew she'd have slept until her midday class, if not for Amelia's insistence.

"What are you doing, anyway?" Amelia slid lipstick over her mouth while she waited for Penny to answer. "Hot date with Cisco?"

Penny spluttered. "Hot date? Why does everyone keep assuming we're dating? No! I'm job-hunting."

"Hon, you know my parents are loaded. Anything you want, I'll buy for you. Well, my dad will buy it for you." Amelia blotted her makeup.

"I'd be a kept woman," Penny joked. "I'm not that kind of girl. You know that."

"I know." Amelia pulled Penny into a hug, her hair clouding around them, and the scent of her makeup heavy in the air. "But still, the offer is there if you need it."

"Thanks, Amelia." Although Penny had no intention of taking Amelia up on her offer, it comforted her to know that in an absolute emergency, she had someone to count on.

Hsss. Boots, unhappy with the lack of attention, flicked her tail and disappeared into the crumpled blanket in the corner.

"Sorry, lovely." Penny shoved a hand into the pile and grabbed Boots, who'd gone as limp as wet spaghetti. "But if you're going to throw a wobbly, I'm not taking you to breakfast."

At the word "breakfast," Boots immediately perked up. She wrapped herself around Penny's arm and slithered around her shoulders, settling in for a comfortable ride.

"Any more of that attitude and I'll make you walk," Penny cautioned.

Boots licked her ear.

"And stop sucking up. You're better than that!" Penny grabbed her smaller bag, threw in a notebook, pen, and her purse, and slipped her phone into her pocket. "Do you have time to eat, Amelia?"

"Alas, no." Amelia pressed the back on her hand to her forehead. "I shall have to weather the famine on nothing but a handful of air and the image of the dastardly handsome Professor McClure to nourish me."

"I wouldn't let Red hear you talk like that!" Penny warned.

Amelia erupted into laughter. "He agrees!"

"You two are *crazy!*" She waited for Amelia to step out into the hallway and pulled the door shut behind them. "Good crazy, but still. Crazy."

By the time Penny saw Amelia again, she had three pages of prospective job ads noted down, had sent her resume to twelve companies, and had filled out nine online applications. She took a seat in Advanced Mythology and pressed her fingers to her eyes.

"Brains falling out?" Cisco asked sympathetically.

Penny nodded. "I really shouldn't spend three hours web surfing on a tiny phone."

Cisco ducked his head as Professor Madera entered and whispered, "Why didn't you use the library?"

Penny grimaced and pointed to her back. As if sensing the motion, Boots peeked out, her eyes dreamy and relaxed. "Because *someone* was intent on eating herself into a food coma."

"Penny, I've told you before," Amelia said, taking a seat nearby. "Three plates is more than enough!"

"Shut up, you." Penny leaned over and gave her a shove, but quickly sobered when Professor Madera coughed for attention.

Rather than start the lesson, the professor looked at her watch and then the door. She glanced at the watch again... and finally, the door opened.

Agent Crenel whipped through, his loose tie and unbuttoned cuffs giving an extra layer of urgency to his deep frown.

"Good morning, students." He dipped his head respectfully to Professor Madera. "Thanks for letting me take over for a few minutes."

Crenel walked over to the whiteboard and slapped a newspaper article up, pinning it in place with two magnets. Two rows from the back, Penny couldn't make out the headline.

"Most of the content in your course has been focused on the supernatural element to this threat," Crenel said, his voice easily carrying through the silent class. "Unfortunately, that's not all we have to contend with. Is everyone aware of the events leading up to the Kraken incident?"

A mutter spread through the room. "Some of us didn't get the inside scoop," Mara said. "Are we allowed to know what happened?"

Crenel scanned the room. "Yes. I'll see those case files are distributed to everyone by the end of the day. Our focus right now, however, is on *why* the event occurred. The Kraken's appearance was instigated by humans." Crenel, now deep into his briefing, began to pace across the classroom. "A man named Tobias was given a spell by a group of terrorists."

Penny heard the collective gasp. Despite already knowing the sequence of events intimately, she still felt the gut-punch of knowing that the monster had been deliberately called.

"Great," Jason said. "Now the bad guys have weaponized spells."

"A human with a spell is still less of a threat than an angry mega-squid," Crenel reassured him. "But, yes. They have weaponized spells."

"But they're human," Mara pointed out. "Aren't there regular cops who can take care of that?"

"You want a beat cop to walk into a coven full of witches summoning a demon?" Crenel asked. "Because that happened. The beat cop ended up spread across two blocks. They spent a week collecting his intestines."

Penny's gut roiled, and more than one student coughed in disgust. Mara whimpered and looked down at her desk.

"That's why we're training you. To deal with the kind of threats they can't. But you need to know that it's not always going to be a god or a specter causing the threat. It could be a guy with a Mythological weapon. Or it *could* be a god or a specter, but with human influence behind it." Crenel plucked the newspaper back off the wall fast enough that the magnets holding it didn't move. He passed it to Mara in the front row to read and pass on. "Primarily, this is presenting in the form of groups calling themselves covens. We call them what they are—*cults*."

Crenel gave a quick explanation of Tobias's cult. He glossed over details of the Eastern group Tobias had met with, simply calling it a "work in progress" and saying that any real information was classified.

"That's two groups," Jason said. "How many are there?"

Crenel lifted his hands. "You tell me. The organizations we've come across so far number in the hundreds. They range from highly organized terrorist cells to the more commonly found groups of casual Wiccans dancing around a fire. We've seen high school students, lawyers, grandmothers, and even some of our own."

"The FBI is summoning monsters?" Mara sounded shocked.

Crenel waggled his hand. "Not successfully, and not necessarily monsters. Many of the groups trying to pull entities through the veil are simply looking to strengthen their religion or just have some fun. Which isn't to say it isn't dangerous, but their *intent* isn't to harm anyone."

"Is it legal?" Cisco asked.

Crenel raised his hands. "For the most part. If we can't get them on a charge based on intent to disrupt the peace or deliberately cause harm to others, then our hands are basically tied. Lawmakers are scrambling to deal with it, but finding a solution that's broad enough to cover all reasonable possibilities—and that doesn't infringe on people's basic rights—is harder than it looks."

"That's what we'll be dealing with when we graduate?" Clive tapped his desk impatiently. "Teenagers and soccer moms trying to conjure house fairies?"

"In some cases," Crenel admitted. "But there is a lot of dangerous stuff out there and not enough people to deal with it yet. Depending on your chosen career paths, many of you will face danger. You will be put into positions where you must risk your lives to save others. And for some of you, it may not wait until graduation."

Penny met the agent's eyes and shivered. She knew that she and Cisco could be called up for a mission at any time since both had chosen the fieldwork career path.

Crenel quickly wrapped up his briefing, telling the students he would be a frequent presence at the Academy to make sure the dean was kept up to date with the latest developments. He passed the class back over to Professor Madera.

"Well, students." Madera pressed her mouth into a thin line. "Let us hope that the next years pass quickly for us, and slowly for everyone else. We will need as much of a head start as we can get. Now, please open your books to page three-hundred and sixty-five."

Sweat dripped down Penny's nose and dropped to the floor. She grunted, shoving herself back up on aching arms.

"Backs straight!" Professor Glass barked. "Mara, out. Eighty-eight. Eighty-nine. Red, you're out. One hundred and Ninety."

Penny's shaking arms collapsed, and she hit the floor. Glass barked her name, and she scrambled to her feet and took her position against the wall, watching the final students on the floor. Jason was called next. He'd managed two hundred and twenty push-ups before he collapsed.

Cisco lifted his head just long enough to see Clive was still going beside him. Both of them were shirtless, biceps and backs rippling as they dipped and rose.

Penny, however, only had eyes for one. She didn't look away even when Amelia nudged her.

"Hot in here, isn't it Penny?" she teased.

"Amelia, you didn't even make it to triple digits," Penny pointed out. "You've had plenty of time to cool off."

Cisco was up to two hundred and forty-one. His arms had begun to tremble, and sweat ran down his back and face. Somehow, he still had the energy to glance at Penny and wink.

"Forty-two. Clive, out," Glass barked. "Two-forty-three."

Cisco dipped again, hesitated, then pushed back up with an audible groan. On his two hundred and forty-fifth, he dipped too low, and his forehead touched the floor.

"Done!" The eagle-eyed Glass had seen the contact. He tossed Cisco a towel and a bottle of water. "I guess that was an acceptable effort." He slid his eyes to Amelia. "For some of you."

"Good effort, bro." Clive clapped Cisco's shoulder. "I'll get you next time, though."

"You almost had me this time," Cisco admitted, still panting. "I'm gonna hurt tomorrow."

"Then it's a good thing you have until Thursday to recover," Glass said. He ignored the students' groans. "Whoever the hell trained you last semester did one hell of a bad job. You're behind, and it shows. I'll have you caught up in no time, but yes, it'll hurt to get there."

"Why is this a mandatory class?" Trevor had bowed out not long after Amelia. "I'm going to be stuck in a lab all day, not fighting Olympiads."

"And when you open a locked relic and something

jumps out?" Glass pointed at Trevor. "It's always the weak ones who don't see the point. Physical fitness is more than just fighting off monsters. It's about mental strength, too. It's about treating your body like a temple so that it serves you instead of failing you when you need it most."

"Hey, I'm not complaining." Trevor raised his hands defensively. "I think we can all agree that I'm no specimen of physical prowess."

Glass grinned. "That's my man. I'll have you looking like an Olympian by the time this semester is done." His smile fell away. "Even if it kills you."

Trevor gasped, and Glass chuckled. "I'm messing with you, kid. I'm not gonna kill you. You'll probably wish I had a few times, but you'll survive."

Penny felt buoyed by the professor's zeal. Since moving to Portland, she'd gotten soft. In Larribee, the only source of entertainment was the local gym and socializing usually meant helping out on a nearby farm.

Now? Her days consisted of endless coffee while her ass was glued to a chair studying.

Glass would whip her into shape in no time, and Penny was looking forward to the challenge.

Wednesday morning arrived. Penny threw herself out of bed. She'd been looking forward to this particular class all week, or, more specifically, to meeting the instructor.

Professor Quaid hadn't been seen since the welcome dinner. Cisco told Penny the former agent was still in the process of moving to the state after giving up retirement in some far corner of the country.

The idea of meeting Agent Crenel's teacher and mentor fascinated Penny. She was quickly realizing that the agent embodied much of what she aimed for. Crenel was dedicated to the cause, but he wasn't so indoctrinated that he couldn't think for himself.

Even his grumpy nature appealed to Penny; the idea that one could work for the government without being a total kiss-ass made the idea sound more attractive than it otherwise would have.

Penny arrived at Weapons class early. She knocked on the classroom door and, when no one answered, she pushed it open.

No one was there.

She took a seat near the front and pulled her books out, looking up when the door opened again. Cisco gave her a quick wave and took the seat next to her.

"Where's Red?" Penny asked. The two were usually inseparable, at least when Amelia wasn't around.

"I left him in the dining hall," Cisco answered. "I wanted to get here early to see what Quaid is like. Can't believe they found someone even older than Crenel!"

"Crenel isn't *that* old," Penny said. "He's... like a grandpa. Not a dinosaur. Not yet, anyway."

"Quaid probably cut his teeth hunting mammoth." Cisco fished around in his bag and drew out a basic exercise book and a pencil. He examined the broken tip. "Hey, do you have a—"

Penny slid a pen across his desk before he even finished asking. "Don't lose it," she warned.

The classroom door opened again. Clive and Mara stepped in and, behind them, Professor Quaid.

Gray hair stuck out of his head at odd angles, and he hadn't shaved since Penny had first glimpsed him at the dinner. His tie was crooked, and creases lined his sleeves.

Quaid unpacked a leather messenger bag, carefully setting the books and pens on his desk and lining them up meticulously. By the time he'd finished setting up, the rest of the students had arrived and found their seats.

"Looks like you're all here," Quaid said gruffly.

Penny glanced around the room. She didn't see a single person who wasn't giving Quaid their whole attention. Clearly, she wasn't the only student looking forward to weapons class.

"Who here has fired a weapon before?" Quaid asked.

Penny raised her hand, as did Clive and Jason. After a minute, Kathy put hers up too.

Quaid nodded. "Well, forget anything you've been taught. We're going to start from the beginning."

Penny filled about twenty pages during the lesson, noting down different gun types and their uses. She listed the rules of training and safety instructions and jotted down questions she wanted to ask in the margins.

Of course, there were some questions she couldn't ask. "How can I learn to be a badass?" wasn't something an Academy professor was likely to answer, even if they could. However, Penny was quickly realizing that she wanted what Agent Crenel had: respect, authority, and the capacity to save the world.

Penny turned her attention back to agent Quaid. He was wrapping up the class, eyes already darting toward his wristwatch. At exactly half-past eleven, he set down the red laser pointer he'd used on the slides he'd shown the class.

"That's it for today." Quaid gave the class a dismissive wave. "You can stop gawking. Go on, go get drunk, or whatever teenagers do between classes these days. Scram!"

A burst of activity erupted as the students around Penny quickly packed up their books and pencils and left the classroom. Penny ignored them, carefully packing away her things one by one.

As the bustle of movement receded, Boots peeked out of her hiding spot.

"There you are," Penny said. "You haven't come out to say hello once today. Were you sleepy?"

Boots tasted the air with a flickering tongue and nosed Penny's books. A shadow crossed over her, and she looked up into the wondering face of Professor Quaid.

"Are you the girl with the lizard?" he asked.

Penny tipped her head to one side, bemused. "She's a rainbow serpent, and that's my bag she is in. So...yes?"

Quaid lifted a sardonic eyebrow. "Looks like a normal snake to me. A regular python. It's not unusual to keep one as a pet. Crenel told me she's a Myther, though."

Penny started. "You can't see them?" She didn't ask the obvious question: why would the academy of myths and legends employ a professor who couldn't *see* myths and legends?

"Of course, I can't damn well see them. What do I look like, some kid with my head in the clouds?" Quaid shook his head. "They tell me it takes a certain kind of mind to see them once you're past your early twenties. Some have gained the ability after a sudden exposure in life-threatening circumstances, but I've been out of the Bureau for five years now, so that ain't gonna happen." He shrugged. "But I don't need to be able to see fairies and unicorns to teach you how to hit a target or run a stakeout. I'm good at what I do and not much else."

Penny stammered an apology, but the professor waved it off. "Don't go making a fool of yourself, kid. I'll teach you to shoot, and you watch my back. If one of these kids gets an idea in their head involving a poltergeist and a bag of confetti, at least give me a warning. Agreed?"

"That's a very...specific deal," Penny said, her eyes narrowed. "Have you ever *met* a poltergeist with a bag of confetti?"

"If I told you, I'd have to kill you. I doubt your Dean would have any hesitation in sharing the story, though." Quaid gave her a quick wink and strode out of the classroom.

Penny quickly packed up the last of her things. "We're gonna have to look out for that one," she told Boots. "Not just for our own sake. If he can't see Mythers, we'll have to be his eyes."

Boots slowly nodded her head. Though the snake was sometimes obstinate and feigned otherwise, she could follow almost any instruction Penny gave her. That she was clever enough to respond only reinforced Penny's conviction that one day, they might be able to communicate.

Penny grinned at Boots. "Come on. Let's go get some grub. We don't have long until the next class."

CHAPTER FIVE

Professor Anand's melodious voice rang out above the scratching of pencils on paper as the students frantically took notes. "Despite originating thousands of miles apart and with entire oceans separating them, the stories told through history often mimic each other in ways that transcend mere coincidence."

"You mean like creation myths?" Kathy asked.

"That," Anand agreed. "But so much more. Take, for example, the wendigo. It's one I assume you are all familiar with?"

A murmur of assent went through the classroom.

Penny timidly raised her hand. "It's just a big beast like a Sasquatch, right?"

The Wendigo wasn't a creature that any of her professors had covered in class, and it wasn't a myth she knew much about.

Professor Anand waggled her hand. "The Sasquatch, Yeti, and Bigfoot are all quite similar. The Wendigo is an overgrown beast, yes, but it comes from stories told by some Native American tribes. The Algonquian peoples, specifically. Clive, tell us what you know about this particular myth."

Clive jumped, looking around as if just realizing he was in the classroom. "Um, which myth was that?"

"The Wendigo," Anand said dryly.

Clive screwed up his face in concentration. "It's Native American. He's really tall and skinny, I think it's meant to symbolize greed or gluttony. He is a cannibal. Wait, he's not human, but he eats humans. Does that make him a cannibal?"

"No, you doofus," Mara called. "You're only a cannibal if you eat your own kind."

"Many of the myths agree the Wendigo began as human," Professor Anand clarified. "That would indeed make him a cannibal. He eats the flesh of humans, but each time he ingests a meal, his body grows. That means he can never be satisfied; he is always craving."

"Like Baba Yaga?" Jason asked. "She tried to eat that Ivan guy. Or one of her sisters did, anyway."

Anand whirled, jabbing a triumphant finger at him. "Exactly! Through all of history, cultures have stories about cannibalism. Lamias, Baba Yaga, the Wendigo, the Hansel and Gretel witch, Kronos, the *wechuge*. Our fascination with it doesn't end there. Apart from Hannibal Lector, how many horror movies have you all seen that feature cannibalism?"

"They're not exactly the same, though," Cisco pointed out. "The fat witch in the candy cottage is a far cry from a skinny giant who eats children."

"In this particular myth, the commonality is the behavior." Anand walked up to the board at the front of the class and scrawled 'behavior' on one side. She underlined it. "There are other myths that present visual commonalities."

On the other side of the board, Anand wrote "aesthetic." "Who can give me an example of that?"

"Zeus and Odin?" Kathy asked.

"Yes, and don't you think both of them look like many of the depictions of the Christian God?" Anand asked. She then walked back to the board and drew circles around each of the two words, large enough that they overlapped in the middle. "Let's take two more examples. Jesus Christ and Hercules. What do they share?"

"They both have long hair?" Clive called.

Anand raised a single eyebrow.

Before she could answer him, Kathy called out. "They're both descended from a god and a human."

Anand smiled. "Correct!" She centered the word "Origin" beneath the other two words. The circle she drew around it created a Venn diagram.

"And some myths are alike in every way," Penny said, guessing what was to come next.

Anand grinned and raised her hands. "Such clever students. This class may be easier than I anticipated."

"So, how does this translate to what's happening today?" Cisco asked. "If the witch from Hansel and Gretel appeared, would she be linked with a Wendigo?"

Professor Anand sighed dramatically. "This, Cisco, is something we have yet to determine. At this point, it seems as though each entity that crosses to our world is its own identity, based on the myth it sprang from. The problem is that it muddies the water when attempting to identify some of these creatures. Take for example the Yeti, the Sasquatch, and Bigfoot."

"I'd rather not take one on ever again," Red muttered.

Anand pointed at him. "Yes, I did hear about that unfortuitous event last semester. Do you know, however, which of the three you captured?"

Penny frowned. "It wasn't a Yeti, because it wasn't white," she said.

"How many people know that a Yeti should be white?" Anand countered. "Some of these creatures are born from mass belief. Although we now have the technology to instantly research and disseminate information, that is only a recent development. For too many years, our only method of sharing such information was the written word, and before that, stories. Both of those were quite limited, especially in times where travel was difficult."

"So, if enough people believed a Yeti could appear in Oregon and didn't know that Yetis are supposed to be white..." Cisco shook his head, face crinkled with confusion. "What *did* it turn out to be?"

Anand shrugged. "The jury is still out. Although the creature you caught shares aspects most common with a Bigfoot, there is enough ambiguity between it and the Sasquatch that there is no definitive way to tell. The chance remains, however small, that it could, indeed, be a misrepresented variation of the Yeti myth, although I personally doubt it is likely."

"But the Yeti lives in the Himalayas," Kathy said. "How could it appear here?"

"Bacchus came to dinner the other night, and I'm pretty sure this isn't ancient Greece," Cisco shot back. "And the influx of leprechauns should be confined to Ireland going by that logic."

"Are we just gonna completely gloss over the fact that there could be a full-grown Wendigo out there stalking the streets?" Clive called. "How is that not scaring the shit out of everyone?"

"I understand your terror," Anand said sardonically. "But please watch your language inside of my classroom."

Clive mumbled an apology.

"It is a terrifying prospect," Anand conceded. "But thankfully, you have classes that will teach you to deal with such threats. In this space, we only discuss ideas."

Despite Professor Anand's reassurance, goosebumps ran over Penny's flesh. In the six short months she had been studying at the Academy, none of the horrors she had encountered quite matched up to a towering, cannibalistic monster.

Let's just hope that one stays theoretical, she thought. Pushing it out of her mind, she bent her head and continued scribbling notes.

Within a few weeks, it was as if Penny had never left the Academy. The new instructors worked their students hard, and the increased schedule, especially now their physical training had stepped up a gear, was tiring, but Penny never lost the buzz of excitement she felt on her first day.

Of all her classes, advanced driver training was her favorite. Professor Blaisey, or "Mack," as he insisted the students call him, was a hot-headed millionaire with a passion for driving. Penny got the impression it was an effort for him to hold back his recklessness, something that she, Cisco, Clive, and Jason kept pushing him to embrace.

"You're driving today, aren't you?" Amelia asked as Penny pulled a shirt over her head.

"Yeah. It's Friday." Penny reached for her jeans.

"I didn't know because it's Friday, I know because you've got that look." Amelia smirked.

"Look?" Penny hesitated, one leg in her jeans and one out.

Amelia rolled her eyes. "That look you get whenever you get to go hurtling around that racetrack. Admit it, you love the thrill."

"Damn right, I do!" Penny quickly finished dressing and pulled her hair into a low ponytail. She glanced at Amelia's bed, stacked with neat piles of clothes. "Oh, shit. It's Friday!" Friday was the day the four friends were leaving Portland for a three-day beach party. It was, like most social events Penny was invited to, hosted by a friend of Amelia's.

Amelia snorted. "And you haven't packed. You're as bad as those boys, Penny!"

Grinning, Penny shrugged. "I can't deny it. I only have ADT today, though. I can shoot back and put some things together as soon as class is over. Do I need to bring anything special?"

"Something sexy, something warm, and something to get the sand outta your butt." Amelia collapsed into giggles at her own joke.

"Right." Penny grabbed her coat. "Will you be here when I get back?"

"Most likely." Amelia shooed her out of the room, Boots twitching under Penny's blanket at the noise.

"Behave for Amelia, Boots!" It was the one class Penny didn't take her scaled friend to. Boots did okay on car trips, but bouncing around a racetrack wasn't her thing.

Penny raced out, taking the stairs two at a time as she ran for the Academy parking lot, the rendezvous point for the bus that would take the small class to Mack Blaisey's training track.

CHAPTER SIX

"Who wants to take this puppy for a spin?" Mack's eyes twinkled as four hands shot into the air. "I'd tell you to take it one at a time, but, well... Go look for yourselves." He waved at the nearby hangar.

Unable to suppress her grin, Penny turned and sprinted toward the building that held Mack's selection of toys. As far as she knew, all of them were his personal property, from the top-end sports cars to the selection of motorbikes, and even a streamlined black tank.

Her heart thumped an extra beat when she thought of that beast. He hadn't let the students drive it yet, insisting they first familiarize themselves with the controls through a simulator. The first time the students had strapped into the replica cockpit, they'd all managed to land the virtual machine upside down.

Today's treat was a top-of-the-line Jeep with all the bells and whistles. *Come to think of it, I don't think even Jeep sells some of these bells or whistles,* Penny realized.

She reached the hangar door first, unlatched it, and

started pushing against it. Cisco quickly arrived and helped slide it open. They grabbed a suit and helmet each and headed for the Jeeps.

Four sparkling jeeps in different colors sat at the entrance, ready to go. Penny chose the green one; it was quickly becoming her favorite color. She pulled the suit over her clothes.

"What, no pink?" Cisco joked.

"Say the word, and I can make it happen!" Mack called from behind him, the engine of his ATV idling.

"Black is fine," Cisco called back. "Good for hiding in the dark."

"A man who thinks ahead, I like it." Mack waited for the students to climb into the cars.

Penny reached for the ignition and found the keys sitting inside it. She gave it a twist and gunned the engine. She let it idle while she donned her helmet and clicked the comm unit on so she could hear her classmates and instructor. "Testing One."

"Received, Wallaby." Mack had chosen a code name for each student and used it every chance he got.

Penny and Cisco had a secret theory that Mack had always wanted to be a secret agent, and was taking advantage of the idea that this was as close as he would ever get.

Three more voices rang through Penny's speakers, Mack responded to each.

"Let's go!" Mack sped off, heading toward the custom-built track at the back of the former airport. Apparently, he had only purchased the property after the formation of the Academy.

You'd never know it, Penny mused as she watched the speedometer climb.

She was slowly getting used to seeing the speed in miles rather than kilometers. Thankfully, the track was a single lane, and Penny hadn't yet had to wrestle with driving on the wrong side of the road.

Penny pulled the steering wheel to the left as smooth concrete gave way to a rugged dirt track. She hit the first bump slowly, gauging the Jeep's response. She spun around a corner, leaving a cloud of dirt behind her.

She heard Cisco's whoop of joy behind her and let out one of her own in response. Heart racing, she floored the accelerator, and the Jeep flew over one of the jumps. The enclosed helmet and racing harness did nothing to dampen the adrenaline rush.

Ahead, Mack skidded to a stop. Penny pulled up next to him and killed the engine.

The com unit nested in her helmet crackled. "I set out something special for you today." Mack's voice held a hint of eagerness. "Five points for every Zombie you hit. You lose fifty if you hit a kid."

"You've got kids on the course?" Clive asked incredulously.

"Yes, Hotdog. I borrowed a few random toddlers and set them loose. If you kill one, you fail the class rather than be charged with negligent homicide." The dry sarcasm in Mack's voice made Penny giggle.

"Give me a break, man. I've got a cold." Clive sniffed to make his point. "It's made my brain go fuzzy."

Mack lost any sense of joviality. "I don't want to risk you out there if you're not up to it," he said. "Take the course at half speed. You can do it again when you feel better."

There was a moment of silence, and Penny imagined Clive was cursing his poor luck. When the radio crackled back to life, however, he simply thanked their instructor.

"You're welcome, Hotdog. Student safety is paramount, after all. Now, who's going first?" Mack asked.

Penny slammed her gloved fingers on the comm button. "Me!" She knew the system would only let one person speak at a time, so Mack would only hear the person who got in first.

"Pink Ranger wins," Mack said.

Penny cursed, but good-naturedly. Cisco's codename never failed to make her giggle. Besides, she would get her chance.

Mack continued his instructions. "The course hasn't changed in layout, but I've added a few surprises. You've got a five-minute head start, and then I will send the next person. All good?"

"Good to go!" In his excitement, Cisco nearly ruptured Penny's eardrums.

"Can we get some sound limiters in these things?" she asked, laughing.

"And here I thought you'd be the one screaming like a girl," Mack joked. He didn't hear Penny's private outrage since she forgot to press the comm button first.

Cisco rolled up to the white line crossing the dirt track. Through the comm, Penny could hear Mack's breath as he held his speak button. Then, a quick snap of voice. "Pink Ranger... Go!"

Cisco sprayed dirt as he floored the kitted-out Jeep.

The car flew off, and Penny grinned when Mack hooted with excitement.

"Wallaby, you're next!" he called.

Penny put her car into gear and rolled up to the starting line. Her heart pounded with excitement as she waited for the minutes to pass.

"You ready, kid?" Mack asked.

"Hell, yes!" Penny gave the engine a gentle rev.

"Ten seconds... Five. Four. Three. Two. Aaaaand... GO!" Mack yelled the last word.

Penny's stomach flipped as she threw the Jeep into gear.

She took off, swinging the tail of the car a little to one side. "Dammit!" Cisco's start had been perfect. She'd have to make up for that little error on the track.

Penny crested a hill and screamed when a figure popped up at the bottom. "Demon!"

The cardboard cutout looked like a promotional product for *The Walking* Dead—except for some minor crumpling and a black tire mark across its torso.

Penny nudged the wheel to the left and slammed the two-dimensional zombie into the dirt. "Ha!"

Excitement coursed through her veins, along with a hint of worry. Cisco was still ahead.

Penny spun the wheel and drifted around a corner, smoothly regaining control as the track straightened. Two figures stood ahead—one a zombie, the other a yellow-haired girl in a pink dress. *They're so close they're almost touching each other*, she realized.

The girl was on the outside of a corner, the demon just to her right. If Penny swung through on her usual line, she might hit the cardboard child.

Slowing down a little, Penny took the turn. She clipped the demon with the side of the car, missing the child completely.

Penny picked up speed on the straight. She swerved left and right, taking down a zombie farmer and his skeletal dog, then skirting around a child standing bang in the middle of the track.

She rounded the final corner, passing an old, red barn. The finish line was in sight.

Penny reflexively flicked a glance at her mirrors. "Fuck!" She yanked the handbrake and the car spun, coming to a stop facing backward.

Standing in the yawning doorway of the barn, a zombie hung from a rope, dangling nine feet off the ground.

"How the fuck am I supposed to get that one?" Penny scanned the ground and saw the tell-tale shadow of a hidden rise. Chuckling, she gunned the engine.

This time her take-off was perfect. She threw herself into the moment, all her senses focused on the jump, the car, the wind, and the dangling demon.

The car nosed down a dip, and the front tilted up as it hit the jump. The Jeep's tires lost traction, and Penny was airborne.

The Jeep slammed into the spinning cutout, tearing it from the door frame. She slammed forward, then back as the Jeep hit the ground inside the barn in a cloud of dust, jolting her in her seat despite the tightly secured racing harness.

"YEAH!" Penny pumped one fist in the air before circling around the barn and getting back on the track. She slammed a hand on the comm, pressing the button that would patch her into Mack, but not the others; she wasn't giving this little secret away. "Zombie down, Mack! I ripped it from the door frame."

Mack didn't answer, but when Penny passed the barn again, she caught a fresh cutout plunging from the rafters to dangle in the wind.

The man thinks of everything, Penny thought. *Everything!* She sped across the finish line and pulled up next to a morose Cisco.

"Good work," he said.

Penny took off her helmet and shook out her hair. "You missed the last one, didn't you?" She plucked a small earpiece out of it and hooked it over her ear.

Cisco nodded, then put a hand over his ear as the comm crackled.

"Fuck!" Jason yelled. "Fuck, fuck, FUCK! Stupid kid! Where the fuck are her parents anyway? Who lets a four-year-old play in a zombie wasteland unsupervised?"

"Looks like someone hit a kid," Penny said with a chuckle. "Should we tip him off about the hidden mark?"

Indecision crossed Cisco's face for a moment, then he nodded. "He can't beat us, not with a minus-fifty."

Penny slid out of her Jeep and waved Cisco over. "Boost me!" A minute later, she was on the roof of the car, squinting at the blind corner near the end of the track.

She heard him before she saw him. Penny waved her arms, pointing both hands at the open-sided barn. Jason shot around the corner and slowed a little when he saw her. Then, he spun the car around and plunged toward the barn.

His Jeep dipped, rose, and flew. It clipped the dangling

demon's feet, lacking the height to tear it down. The cutout zombie swung wildly but stayed attached to the rope it hung from.

"Ahh, he missed it!" Penny said. Still, she waved a fist and cheered as Jason crossed the finish line.

Mack shouted, "Go!" signaling that Clive was on his way.

Jason pulled his car up next to hers and lifted his helmet off. "Thanks for the tip, guys," he called. "You think it'll count as a hit? I'm pretty sure I nudged it."

"You did," Penny confirmed. She smothered a giggle. "Jason? Check your hair, man. It looks like you've been dragged through a hedge backward!"

With a look of alarm, Jason darted back into his car and used the mirror to smooth down his hair. Once satisfied, he re-emerged. "Hairspray and helmets don't mix."

"You use hairspray?" Cisco asked, sniggering.

"You don't?" Jason retorted. "Never mind. It's pretty obvious that you don't."

Feigning hurt, Cisco patted his curly hair. "Because my head is perfect as it is. Isn't it, Penny?" He turned puppy dog eyes her way.

Penny waved him away. "I'm not getting involved in this. Not a chance!"

The roar of an approaching engine made her turn just in time to see Clive slide around the final corner. Before she had time to react, he'd crossed the finish line. *So much for half speed.* She knew Mack would tear him a new one for that later.

Clive tumbled out of the car and punched the air. "Perfect run!" he yelled.

Penny smirked and shook her head. She pointed at the dangling zombie. "You sure about that?"

Clive spun and let out a deep groan. "Man. Did anyone else get it?"

"Penny ripped it clean off the rope," Cisco informed him. "Jason clipped it, but he hit a kid, too."

"How'd you know that?" Jason asked.

"We heard you cursing about it," Penny told him, laughing. "We figured out what happened pretty easily."

"Oh. I guess I came in last, then. Unless..." He looked at Cisco, who shook his head.

"Sorry, man. I had a pretty clean run. I only missed that last zombie." Cisco accepted a fairly subdued high-five from Jason.

Moments later, Mack pulled up. "Hey, guys! Who won?"

Penny stepped forward. She knew Mack would already know how each student had gone. All of his vehicles were fitted with multiple dash cams that were linked to his phone. She had no doubt he had watched each race as it happened, making notes on where they could improve.

"I did." She couldn't keep the excited grin from her face.

Mack clapped. "Good work, Wallaby!" He cocked his head, a corner of his mouth pulling up in a clever smile. "So, what do you think your prize should be?"

"Prize?" Penny faltered. "What, do I get a certificate or something?"

Mack's eyes slid toward the Jeep.

"Nooo." Cisco's eyes were huge. "You're kidding."

"Not for keeps," Mack quickly clarified. "Just for a week. Sound good?"

"Hell, yes!" Penny said when she found her tongue. "Are you for real?"

"Sure." Mack hopped back into his car. "Just bring it back in one piece. See you next week!" He slammed his door shut, waved, and drove away. Over the intercom, Penny heard his final instruction. "The rest of you can keep the cars until sundown. Enjoy!"

Cisco and Jason let out a whoop of joy, while Clive threw himself back into his own car and strapped in.

"Another round?" Cisco asked.

Penny shook her head. "I have to get back. I haven't started packing yet!"

Cisco cocked his head. "You're... packing? It's only for two days. Throw a spare shirt in a bag and off you go!"

Groaning, Penny turned her back on him. "Men. Seriously, I gotta run."

Cisco called after her. "You're driving, right? I'll tell Mom we don't need to borrow the car if you are."

Penny laughed. "Sure. Just make sure I stick to the right side of the road." So far, she had only driven on Mack's closed-circuit tracks. She held an international driving permit, but she hadn't used it yet.

"Right." Cisco sounded dubious. "I can—"

"Don't say it," she warned.

"Drive?" Cisco finished hesitantly.

Penny threw her middle finger up over her shoulder. "Be back by three or you'll have to walk."

"Dictator!"

Penny ignored his yell, instead turning the Jeep's engine over and carefully turning it around for the airfield exit. She stuck one hand out the window to wave farewell.

Once at the gate, Penny took in a deep breath. She tapped the Academy's address into the inbuilt GPS. Then, careful to stay in the correct lane, Penny edged onto the road.

She made it back without issue, despite a harrowing turn across too many lanes of traffic that left her feeling like she was stuck in the twilight zone and headed into oncoming traffic.

Penny parked in one of the student bays of the car park, then let out a slow sigh of relief, glad she'd taken the car out for the first time alone. Cisco wouldn't have let her live it down if he'd seen how nervous she was.

She dropped the keys into her bag and sauntered into the building, a flush of pride putting a swing in her step. When she passed the grand entryway into the Academy and someone tapped her shoulder, she jumped.

"Agent Crenel!" Penny had been so wrapped up in her thoughts that she hadn't seen him loitering in the foyer.

"Sorry, Penny. I didn't mean to startle you. Do you have a minute?" He glanced around as Penny nodded. "Perhaps not here."

She followed him into one of the nearby offices on the ground floor of the Academy. This one was empty, likely held for one of the many instructors expected to join the school over the next years.

"What happened?" Penny asked.

Crenel raised an eyebrow but didn't question her assumption. "You're going to that party out at Cannon Beach." It was said as a statement, not a question.

Penny bit down on her impatience, knowing Crenel

wasn't one to dally around. "Arcadia beach, actually. That's just south of Cannon, isn't it? We leave tonight."

Crenel frowned. "There have been some suspicious deaths out that way. Nothing concrete yet. Can you keep an eye out for anything unusual?"

Penny nodded again. "Of course, Agent Crenel. What can you tell me?"

He briefed her quickly. "There have been reports of violent deaths in the area. There haven't been any definite indications of Myther involvement, but the bureau has their ears perked."

"We suspect there's a new coven in the area too," Crenel admitted. "Which isn't to say they're involved. Most actual Wiccans we've encountered have been smart enough not to try summoning anything, and for the most part, their intentions are good. It's the covens that cross over into what we're terming as cult activity we have to watch for."

"What do you know about them?" Penny asked.

Crenel shrugged. "Just that they're out there. We're tracking sales of candles, sage, crystals, that sort of thing. There has been an increasing spike in the sales of occult-associated products since the Veil was made public knowledge, and nine times out of ten, that's what it's attributed to."

"Wow." Penny couldn't smother her surprise. "You guys are really on it, aren't you?"

Crenel brushed off her praise. "Regardless, there is something or someone out there causing a lot of trouble. This perp, human or not, is dangerous." His eyes drilled into Penny's. "Do not engage. Really. Don't."

Penny grinned. "Sure."

"I mean, it, Penny! Can I trust you on this?" Before she could answer, Crenel sighed. "Of course, I can't because you're twenty and invincible."

"Excuse me?" Penny snapped. "I turned twenty-*two* just after New Year's, thank you very much."

Crenel grimaced. "So, you can give your absolute, unbreakable word that you will not engage this predator while you're out there?"

Penny hesitated. "Oh. I guess not. See you Monday!"

Leaving the agent shaking his head behind her, Penny darted out of the room, giggling. She knew Crenel probably just sprouted another dozen gray hairs, and she took pride in that.

She ran into Amelia on her way past the dining hall, and the two walked upstairs together.

"Hey, you ready for tonight?" Amelia asked.

Penny shook her head. "I'm going up to pack now. Hey, guess what?"

Amelia's mouth pulled to one side as she thought. "You...I don't know...finally hooked up with Cisco?"

"What" Penny squeaked. "No! I got us a car for the weekend, you numpty!"

"Oh." Amelia grinned. "So you *have* somewhere to finally hook up with Cisco? Even better." She easily ducked the light punch Penny threw at her shoulder. "You know you want to. So, how'd you get a car?"

Penny quickly explained, unable to hide her grin as Amelia gushed over the Jeep and her win. "You utter gem, Penny!" Amelia hugged her before pushing the dorm room door open. "Look at you, kicking all those testosterone-laden boys to the curb."

"I do my best." Penny raised her fist and bumped Amelia's, then leaned down to poke Boots, who was curled up on the bed.

Boots didn't respond, just buried herself tighter in the blankets. Penny stroked her head with a finger, then turned to address the burning question. "Now, do I need my nice boots or my comfortable ones? I don't want the red ones ruined if we're going to be near the water."

Amelia hesitated, and Penny could practically see the cogs turning. With a sigh, Amelia pointed to Penny's old faithfuls. "You're right. Wear those horrible old things."

Penny picked up her work boots and whispered, loud enough for Amelia to hear, "Don't listen to her. You're the *best* boots."

She ignored Amelia's snort of laughter and began throwing clothes into a duffel bag. "How cold is it going to get?"

"For you? Cold. You'll need thick socks and every layer you've got." Amelia giggled. "But then I'd say that if I was only going to take a tank top and shorts. You freeze in the mildest weather!"

"That's true," Penny admitted. "But I'm all kitted out, thanks to you!"

Amelia threw Penny a beanie.

"Where'd this come from?" Penny recognized it as hers, but she hadn't seen it since she'd bought it.

"Found it under my bed while I was looking for those fingerless gloves I wore the other day. You haven't seen them, have you?"

Penny rummaged through the stack of blankets on her bed, to no avail. She got down on her knees. She did find an extra pair of socks, two scarves, a notebook, and a shoe, but no gloves. Penny sat back on her knees. "Sorry, mate. No idea." As she spoke, she tossed the shoe toward the closet in the corner. As it flew, a scrap of pink cloth dislodged from deep inside it.

"My glove!" Amelia shrieked, pouncing on it with glee. "You're awesome!"

"Someone thinks we are." Penny's mind flashed back to her conversation with Agent Crenel. She told Amelia what she knew.

Amelia looked worried for a split second, then broke into a grin. "You really promised not to get involved?"

"Hell, no." Penny mirrored Amelia's grin. "I promised I'd *try* not to."

Amelia pulled a coat out of her overstuffed bag. "Guess we'd better leave room for our kits."

Penny gaped. "You were going to go without one?" Her own Academy-issued travel kit—a small bag with basic weapons and protections—was already packed.

"I was going to take the tiny one, but we're gonna need more than just the basics if something is out there," Amelia told her.

Penny evaluated the still-full bag. "Amelia, there's no way you have room for anything else in there." She smirked. "Apparently, Cisco's only taking a spare shirt. He'll have plenty of space!"

That settled, the two girls quickly finished packing. "Where's your fancy new car?" Amelia asked.

"Student bay," Penny said. She hefted her two bags, mostly packed with thick, warm clothes, blankets, and every sock she owned. She would *not* freeze to death sleeping on a beach. "Let's take these down, then come back for coffee." She dropped an empty knapsack on the bed. "Come on you, unless you're staying behind for the weekend?"

Boots flicked her tail and hissed, but begrudgingly slid into the bag and curled back up. Penny struggled, but she managed to loop all three bags over her shoulders.

Amelia hoisted her own duffel with ease.

Penny had taken little notice of what she'd packed, but she knew that at least some of the outfits would leave her blue and shivering in the current conditions. She envied her friend's tolerance for the cold.

Penny waited by the Jeep, tapping her foot. "I *told* him, if his ass wasn't back by three, I'd go without him."

"He's still got..." Red checked the time on his phone. "Forty-five seconds. He can make it."

At that moment, the front door of the Academy flew open. Cisco raised a fist as he ran toward them, a limp, half-empty backpack dangling from it. "Made it!"

Penny rolled her eyes. "Barely. But seeing as you have so much room in your pack, you're in charge of the monster kit."

Cisco's eyes lit up. "We're taking the monster kit?"

Officially, the Academy had provided three different options of weapon kits for the students to access: the travel kit, issued to each student for daily use; the basic mission kit, a pimped-out version of the basic, and able to be checked out, and the comprehensive field kit, stored in the

Weapons room and only accessible with an official mission ID provided by the FBI liaison.

The students, of course, had already given them names: the leprechaun, the fat leprechaun, and the monster.

"I had to beg for permission," Penny admitted. "But I swung it on the basis that we implement and document at least one example of the surveillance techniques Quaid has been teaching us."

In reality, she'd appealed to Crenel's fatherly nature—what little he had, anyway—by pointing out that two dozen drunk twenty-something kids sleeping on a beach with no protection might attract malicious entities. "What if something attacks in the night?" she'd asked. "And you have to come and ID my body? That would really suck, especially after all the effort you put into recruiting me. Not to mention the torture Dean March would put you through for letting her students come to harm."

He'd still wavered, so Penny had pulled out the big guns. "I mean, just think of the paperwork you'd have to do."

That was when Crenel caved. "Fine. What do you need?"

Penny could feel the agent's scowl through the phone as he rattled off the information she needed to check out the Monster, and was sure she felt his wave of irritation when she ended the call without promising again that she'd avoid —well, try to avoid—a direct confrontation with anything down at Arcadia beach.

Penny popped the trunk and patted the heavy-duty canvas bag. "Amelia and I will have our hands full, dude, so you're in charge of this baby."

Rather than complain, Cisco crowed with delight. "Yeah!" He caressed the duffel, eyes full of wonder. "I'll take good care of you, sweetheart. You won't leave my side. You can even sleep with—"

"Ew!" Amelia shoved Cisco, almost tipping him off balance. "Get a room."

"Are we ready?" Penny waited for Cisco to toss his bag in the back before closing it up. She jingled the keys. "Who's calling shotgun?"

When no one answered, Cisco sighed. He cupped a hand around the back windshield and called, "Goodbye, my love. I have to go and sit up front. I'll miss you!"

"Amelia's right." Penny walked around to the driver's seat and slid behind the wheel. "You have a really unhealthy attachment to that bag." She glanced in the rear-view mirror to see Amelia and Red with their heads together in the back seat. "No canoodling back there! This car is a loaner, and I'm not paying to clean the upholstery when I give it back."

Cisco opened the passenger door and made to shove the small bag on the seat onto the floor. He snatched his hand back when a rainbow head shot out with an irritated hiss.

"Sorry, Boots." He gently picked the bag up and settled it in his lap once his seatbelt was on.

Penny blew out a slow breath as she twisted the keys in the ignition. A troupe of butterflies had taken up residence in her stomach. The trip back from the old airfield had been a few back streets and quiet roads. Now she'd be driving through the city and onto a highway.

Just stay to the right, she reminded herself, then pulled out of the Academy parking lot.

It didn't take long to get used to driving on the other side of the road. After a few miles on the road, Penny had slipped into a comfortable pace. Soon, the bustling city of Portland slipped away as they headed toward the beach with the radio at a low buzz as the friends chattered over the top.

"I really thought Australia was mostly nudist beaches," Cisco insisted.

"You didn't think it, you wished it," Amelia shot back. "I mean, we get tourism ads for down under all the time. No boobs on those at all!"

"Well... Not naked boobs..." Red ducked Amelia's swatting hand.

"You idiot." Amelia folded her arms back up. "You'd chase... wait. What's that *smell*?" She hit Red again, harder. "Was that you? That's disgusting!"

The smell hit Penny in the front, a potent waft that made her eyes water. "Oh, God. Whoever dropped their guts needs to see a doctor about that." She hit the window buttons, trying to air out the car, but it got worse.

Boots struggled out of her bag. She lifted her nose and tasted the air, then dove back inside with an angry hiss.

"Not us," Cisco said in a choked voice. "It's coming from outside. Goddammit, Penny, put the windows back up!"

Coughing hard enough to threaten her lunch, Penny did so. Even sealed off to the outside world the smell persisted. She pressed her sleeve to her nose.

"Smells dead," Red called from the back. "Like, really dead."

One mile on, the odor dissipated as quickly as it had appeared. "That's a relief. I can breathe again!" Penny cracked her window and gave an experimental sniff. "Yup. Definitely gone. I wonder what it was?"

"Boots, you can come out now," Cisco said.

The serpent emerged carefully this time, but once she was satisfied the stench was gone, she lifted her head and rested it on Cisco's arm to watch the scenery pass.

"A body," Amelia suggested. "Of an elephant. Blergh." She slid her own window down and inhaled the now-fresh air. "Hey! I can smell the beach. We must be getting close."

Reports of a car accident holding up traffic on the 101...

"Shut up, guys!" Penny spun the volume dial on the radio. "That's our route."

The car was discovered at six a.m. this morning by a passerby. All occupants were declared dead on the scene, and local law enforcement has cordoned off the roadside stop. We recommend allowing extra travel time if in the area...

The report jumped to an ad for a department store and Penny turned it back down. "Damn. Must have been a bad one."

They didn't hit the worst of the traffic until a few miles later when it slowed to a crawl. Penny turned the radio back up since they promised an hour of ad-free music.

Penny slowed to match the speed of the car in front of her. A staccato beat rang out from the car stereo, and Penny couldn't suppress a grin as *Saturday Night* began to play.

"S.A.T.U.R.D.A.Y." Penny sang the words loudly, grinning when Amelia immediately joined in. "S-S-Saturday *niiiight!*"

Boots reared and hissed loudly, making Penny falter. She turned the music down. "What is it, mate?" Usually, Boots would only react like this if something was wrong.

"Look." Cisco pointed to something on the shoulder of the road ahead. The traffic here was almost to a standstill, and it was a minute before Penny could see ahead to the holdup. When the pulverized car came into view, she killed the music altogether.

"What the fuck?" she whispered. A quick glance in the mirror showed Amelia's eyes wide with horror, too.

The little white sedan had been peppered with fist-sized dents. All of the windows were broken, and the gaping holes in the middle looked like they'd been punched through, rather than shattered by impact. Metal curled in angry shards around a long gash down one side.

Boots writhed uncomfortably, pressing her nose on the glass and making a low rumbling sound.

A car behind her honked, and Penny realized she'd stopped. "Shit." She took her foot off the brake, and the Jeep began rolling forward. Not fast, since even with her momentary distraction, the car in front hadn't gone far.

"That's no crash," Cisco said. "What *did* that?'

The wreck receded in the mirrors as traffic picked up again, and Boots settled back on Cisco's lap, although she still twitched anxiously.

Penny pulled her attention back to the road. "Let's see if we can get any more info." She used her hands-free to make a call.

"Don't tell me I gotta come save your ass already." Crenel's gravelly voice rasped over the car speaker.

"As if." Penny pushed the clutch and changed gears.

"What do you know about the accident on the 101 this morning?"

"Car accident?" Crenel's tone immediately eliminated Penny's hope that he might know something about the incident. "I work for the FBI. I'm not a traffic cop."

"I'm using the term 'accident' loosely," Penny explained. "The car looked like it had been attacked. If you come across anything, keep us in the loop."

"What are you, my boss?" Crenel spoke again before Penny could retort. "Of course, you're not. Even *he* still says please when he asks me to do something."

"Please?" Penny added. "With a cherry on top."

"I'll see what I can do." Penny heard his muffled mutter as he covered the mouthpiece and said something she couldn't make out. "Anything else?"

"Nope. That's all." Penny sniggered. "Unless you want to clean my room for me while I'm gone, subordinate."

"Hilarious." The agent's dry tone suggested he'd found her comment anything but. "I've got shit to do. Try not to get killed out there, okay?"

The beep of an ended call sounded before Penny could reply. She let out a sigh of frustration. "Dammit, I was really hoping he had heard something. If we go back, do you think they'd let us take a look?"

Cisco covered his quick laugh with a cough. "Sure, Penny. All those mean-looking cops back there are going to let us waltz in to investigate with no jobs, no credentials, no authority. What are we gonna tell them? We're not Mystery Incorporated."

"No, we're not," Penny said sadly. "You're nowhere *near* as cute as Scooby-Doo."

CHAPTER SEVEN

Penny shuffled closer to the crackling bonfire, clutching the blanket around her shoulders. Boots curled closer, but the cold-blooded reptile sucked up more heat than she gave.

"There you are!" Cisco's face appeared in the flickering shadows, headed toward her with a drink in each hand. "Here. This will warm you up."

Penny scowled but took the paper cup, keeping it out of easy reach of the curious serpent. "You should be dying of hypothermia right now."

Cisco flexed his bare arms. "I'm acclimatized, that's all. And drunk. *Definitely* drunk."

Penny eyed the amber liquid in the cup. She sniffed it carefully, wrinkling her nose at the sickly sweet scent of rum. "No whiskey?" She was surprised by how much she had grown to enjoy Paddy's favorite drink.

Cisco shook his head. "Sorry. It was that or beer."

Penny shivered. "It'll do, then." She tipped her head back and downed her drink in one go.

"Wow. You Aussies really know how to hit it hard." Cisco took the empty cup off her, scrunched it up and threw it in the fire. It disappeared in seconds, consumed by flames.

"I wish this wind would bugger off," Penny moaned. "Or that the rum would kick in faster. Either will do."

She looked up at Cisco, doing her best impression of puppy-dog eyes. "Walk me back to the Jeep?"

Cisco looped his arm through hers, and they headed back toward the small beachside parking lot. Away from the heat of the fire, the cold bit deeper into Penny's bones. She huddled closer to Cisco.

"What's at the Jeep?" he asked.

"More clothes." Penny had started the afternoon in a light, long-sleeved top. She wished she hadn't listened to Amelia, who had insisted that by the time night fell, the bonfire would be big enough to keep them warm.

"Hey!" Cisco pointed toward the parking lot of the recreation site. One of the vehicles had its interior lights on, and shadows moved inside. "Is that—"

"The Jeep!" Penny dropped Cisco's arm and ran for the borrowed car. She stopped some distance short of it, horrified hand flying to her mouth. She covered her eyes with the other. "Tell me I didn't see what I just saw."

"They're animals!" Cisco said in a low voice. Even at a whisper, he sounded more impressed than horrified. "Not that I expected anything less."

Penny heard grunting and tried very hard to convince herself that she couldn't pick out an Irish accent from the guttural noise. "But that's my *car*! For the week, anyway."

"Are you thinking what I'm thinking?" Cisco said with a grin.

"We shoot them?" Penny suggested hopefully. "And then we rob them blind to cover the cost of steam-cleaning the seats. I'm sure Amelia has at least a few grand worth of shoes."

"Good plan," Cisco said. "But a double homicide and robbery on your record might impact your chances for working for the FBI. Just a hunch."

Penny pouted, rubbing her arms harder. "Then what?"

"Watch." Cisco veered to the left, coming around to the front of the car in a low crouch.

Penny ducked and followed, Boots still dangling over her shoulders. She waited, hidden behind a neighboring vehicle as Cisco crept up to the back door of the Jeep. He flashed a grin, his white teeth sparkling in the moonlight, then pounced and slammed both hands against the car window, letting out a loud roar.

Amelia shrieked and Red screamed, then the passenger door flew open and the two scrambled out.

Penny had to lean against the car she'd hidden behind, she was laughing so hard. Even Boots looked like she was enjoying the spectacle.

"You bastard!" Amelia yelled. She hurled a piece of clothing at Cisco.

He held it up, and Penny almost fell over when she realized it was a lacy red bra. "Are you sure you don't need this?"

Amelia, who despite the lack of lingerie was still wearing a shirt, threatened him with a clenched fist.

"You're lucky I can't reach my bag right now, or you'd be wearing a knife in your eye socket."

"I can't believe you did that," Red moaned, buttoning his jeans. "We were just getting to the good part."

Amelia slapped him on the back of the shoulder. "*You* might have been. I was miles off!"

"Oh, my God, stop!" Penny clapped her hands over her ears. "I swear to God, if there's jizz on that seat…"

"There's not," Amelia hurriedly assured her.

"Thanks to Cisco," Red muttered. He ducked another slap from his girlfriend. "What are you doing here, anyway?"

"All my shit is in there," Penny reminded them. "I'm freezing, and I need my coat." She narrowed her eyes, remembering where she'd left it. "If there's jizz on my coat…"

"Can you *stop* saying 'jizz?'" Amelia dove back into the car and emerged with Penny's jacket. "Look. Perfectly clean."

Penny gingerly took it from Amelia, holding it between two fingers. She gave it a quick examination before slipping it on. "I don't know whether to be grossed out that you were humping on it or glad that it came prewarmed."

Amelia flashed a sunny smile. "You're welcome."

"We'll leave you two to get back to it," Cisco said.

"The hell we will." Penny glared at the offending couple. "There's a whole beach out there. Can't you go bump uglies somewhere…I don't know, less upholstered?"

"And get sand in me crack?" Red shook his head. "No way."

"And now I've got the image of Red's ass stuck in my

head." Cisco threw his hands up in defeat. "I didn't think this night could get any worse. "

A panicked scream filled the air. Boots immediately slithered down, eyes bright, tongue seeking any indication of danger.

"You *had* to say it," Amelia said. She jerked the back door of the Jeep open again. "I've got a mini-kit ready to go. Cisco, grab the monster."

Cisco jumped into action, popping the trunk and hauling out the black duffel bag. The zipper rasped as he pulled it open and handed a handgun to each of his friends. "Amelia, take the crossbow. Penny, do you want the big knife or the little one?"

"Little one. And a solar flare, knuckle dusters, and my yellow beanie."

Cisco tossed her the first three items and a gun belt. He stuck his head back in and popped out a moment later with the knitted beanie. "All set!"

Penny hesitated, looking toward the moonlit road where the scream had come from. On the other side, a thick forest beckoned. An eerie silence reigned, completely devoid of all the sounds one would expect from the woods at night-time.

She took a breath and clipped on her belt. "Okay, Boots." The serpent had her eyes fixed on a point in the darkness, her tongue flicking anxiously as she tasted the air. "Lead the way."

As if she'd been waiting for the command, Boots jumped forward. She slithered through the small car park of the recreation point and onto the Road. Penny nervously glanced in each direction but saw no sign of an approaching vehicle.

As if sensing Penny's caution, Boots made a frustrated clicking sound. She didn't stop, though, quickly crossing the road and disappearing into the bushes on the other side.

"Slow down," Penny called a loud whisper. She swung her flashlight in a wide arc. "Dammit, Boots. Where did you go?"

A hiss by her ear made Penny jump. She berated the snake, who was hanging from a nearby branch. "Are you *trying* to scare the shit out of me?"

When Boots gave a cough that sounded suspiciously like a chuckle, Penny nearly fell on her ass. She rounded on Cisco, thrusting a finger up at him. "That's your fault," she said. "You're a terrible influence!"

He held his hands up defensively. "It was funny!"

Shaking her head, Penny turned back. She quickly picked out the snake making her way down the nearby tree and across the leaf litter scattered on the ground.

Boots hesitated, arching her head up and baring her fangs silently.

Penny pulled her pistol from its holster. She'd only used it at the nearby range where Quaid had been training the students. For the first time, she wished it was a little bigger.

Twigs crackled underfoot as the four Academy students moved through the trees. Dead leaves and spindly branches made it almost impossible to move silently. Overhead, the swollen moon filtered through the leaves to cast long-fingered shadows on the ground.

"This doesn't feel like a B-grade horror movie at all,"

Red muttered. He waved his flashlight at the branches above, then yelped, "I take it back! By the love of all that's holy, I take it back."

Penny lifted her own flashlight up to see the bundle of leaves twirling in the breeze. She squinted. They weren't leaves; the bundle of sticks had been secured with strings to look like little arms and legs sticking out at odd angles. A shiver went down her spine.

"I think I've seen this movie," she said. Her voice was hoarse with fear. "I didn't like it very much."

A twig crackled behind her and she jumped, only for Amelia to slip a hand into hers.

"I'm not scared," Amelia whispered. The whites of her eyes begged to differ. "I'm not. Just...dammit. I'm scared."

"Well, I'm fecking scared," Red hissed back. "I'm telling you now, if some hag with three teeth and a pointy hat jumps out of the trees, I'm going to piss my pants." He glared at Cisco.

"Shh." Cisco crept further forward, motioning for them to follow. He pointed at a shadowy hump on the ground. "Someone had a fire here." He edged closer, holding his hand out. "It's cold. It doesn't look that old, though."

Boots circled around the abandoned campfire, her body seeming longer in the twisted shadows. She arched again, her body frozen except for the slightest twitch in her tail. She hissed, a drawn-out sound that scared Penny almost as much as the twig-dolls in the trees.

Penny held a hand up to the others, pointing her gun in the direction Boots faced.

Something crashed in the darkness. Boots launched herself toward it, disappearing into the shadows.

Silence fell again. It was broken by a low growl.

"Wendigo," Amelia whimpered. "I bet it's a fucking Wendigo."

"You don't know that, pet. Might just be a stray dog." Red didn't sound like he was convinced, though. "A really big stray."

"Boots?" Penny kept her voice low, but anxiety made it strained. "Boots, where are you?"

Silence.

Then chaos.

Sound exploded from the trees, crashing and barking as a creature as tall as Penny burst from the darkness, its yellow teeth dripping with saliva as they snapped at the skinny beam of light from Cisco's flashlight.

"Boots!" The serpent was wrapped around the wolfish neck, slowly constricting as the beast twisted its head, trying to bite her.

Penny let off two rounds. Both bullets hit the dog's chest, safely away from her serpentine friend.

It didn't even flinch.

"That's no dog!" Red yelled. He ejected the chamber of his gun and grabbed a cartridge from the pack at his belt. "Get the silver!"

Silver. Werewolf! The realization sent Penny into a spin as she hastily tried to swap her bullets over. In the darkness, she fumbled the magazine's release, dropping her regular ammunition on the ground. *Fuck it, they won't help me here.*

The wolf—the *were*wolf—dove onto its back, giant paws scratching at its neck. Boots let out a pained hiss and released her grip before darting into the bushes.

The wolf eyed Penny and let out a low growl, hackles raised.

"Hey! Puppy want a bone?" Amelia taunted the dog, and it leaped, sailing over Penny's head as her magazine snapped into place. Penny fired three quick rounds, the loud shots echoed as a nearby muzzle flashed.

The wolf slammed into Amelia, and she screamed.

Penny's heart lurched as her friend was knocked back into the dirt. She heard a loud yell, then saw Red tackle the werewolf and pull it away from Amelia.

Slipping a knife from her belt, Penny dove toward them. She couldn't risk a shot while Red wrestled the creature, but perhaps she could wound it enough to separate them.

She threw herself onto the monstrous wolf and plunged her knife into its side. Teeth snapped at her hand and she yanked it back, leaving the knife still embedded in the thick fur and sinewy muscle.

Two muffled shots went off, and suddenly, the werewolf stilled. Sticky liquid, black under the moonlight, bubbled at the corners of its mouth. It collapsed to one side, flesh writhing as it changed.

The long wolf muzzle shortened, stilling somewhere in between man and beast. The fur thinned, drawing into the skin to leave nothing more than the wiry, sparse hair of a human. The legs shortened, and the fingers lengthened even as the claws began to retract.

Penny winced as the face contorted. *That must hurt when you're not dead.* The resulting face was elongated with a flat nose but otherwise looked like a man.

Amelia pressed a hand to her mouth, scrambling away from the fallen body. "It's…human?"

"Only half." Penny shoved herself away from the man-wolf and stood on shaky legs. She nudged it with a toe. "It hasn't changed all the way back. And if it's a Myther, it's not really human."

Amelia didn't look convinced. "I guess."

"Everyone ok?" Cisco asked.

Red gave a hollow laugh. "Aye. Nothing but a scratch." He held up his arm a thin line of blood welled, but not enough to drip. "Lucky it wasn't a bite, hey?"

"Amelia?" Penny reached to help Amelia up from where she crouched on the forest floor.

"I'm okay." She took Penny's proffered hand and pulled herself up. "But I think from now on, I'm officially a cat person."

Cisco was already pushing through the forest, headed deeper into the trees. "Guys! Come and look at this."

Penny gave a nervous glance at the ground. Two glassy black eyes stared back lifelessly.

Ahead, a gentle glow shone from a small hollow in the ground. The cool light bounced as Cisco nudged it with a foot. "Battery lantern," he said. "Someone is here."

"Hello?" Amelia called out. "The wolf is dead. You're safe now."

Nothing.

Cisco picked up the lantern and held it up. "Uhh, guys? Maybe it's not so safe here. Not for us, anyway."

A flat rock sat nestled among the tall pines. It looked to Penny like it had been naturally placed—settled deep within the soil and leaf litter, no different to the other rocks scattered around.

No different, except for the crudely painted runes that decorated its sides and mounds of candle wax piled around blackened wicks.

"It's some kind of altar." Penny pointed her flashlight at it and took a few steps closer. "Look, that wax hasn't set properly. Guys, I think this is *fresh*."

Immediately, her companions turned their flashlights toward the surrounding trees. Cisco edged closer with the discarded lantern. "What do you think they were trying to summon? The wolf?"

"Unless the altar belongs to the werewolf." Penny ran her fingers through the loose scatter of leaves around the altar. She wasn't sure exactly what she was looking for. A tuft of dog hair, perhaps. An old tooth, maybe even a fragment from a spellbook.

Instead, she found something that made her stomach turn. "This must be from the coven Crenel was talking about."

"It looks like a piece of bandage," she said, picking it up gingerly between two fingers. "Is that…blood?"

"Penny, don't touch it." Amelia swung her flashlight back toward them. "It could be full of diseases."

"Amelia, I think a few germs are the least of our worries." Cisco picked up a stick from the ground and held it out so that Penny could lay the strip of cloth over it.

She wiped her hands on her jeans uncomfortably. "She might be right, Cisco. That thing could be harboring anything from hepatitis to the black plague. Or lycanthropy. Don't touch it, not until we know what we're dealing with."

Amelia unzipped the pouch at her belt. She ran her fingers over the neatly arranged bulges within it. "Here." She slid a tiny white packet from one of the loops and unfolded it to reveal a plastic bag. She held it open so that Cisco could drop the bandage into it and sealed it, shuddering dramatically. "All done. It's safe to breathe again. Oh, and you guys can use this for your surveillance class! If nothing else, you got your homework done, right?"

"Do you think whoever was lurking around here is the person who screamed?" Penny asked. "More to the point, should we be calling in back up?"

Cisco nodded. "Agent Crenel *and* the dean will have our asses if we don't call this in. I mean, we just killed a freaking werewolf."

Penny looked around the area. Apart from the recently used altar, nothing else seemed out of place. Still, something didn't sit right. "Cisco, do you really think the werewolf was responsible for the attack on that car?"

He shrugged. "What else would it be?"

Penny shook her head. "Nothing, I guess. Never mind." The glow of her phone screen made her squint as her eyes adjusted to the bright light. "Damn, I've got almost no reception." She stretched her arm out, holding the phone as high as she could and was rewarded with an extra bar. Penny tapped Crenel's name and put it on speaker.

Crenel's voice was heavy with sleep. "You'd better have a good reason for waking me up at two AM."

Before Penny could answer, she heard a second voice murmuring into the phone.

"Of course they would have a good reason. Don't be a fool, Stuart."

Something about hearing the always-professional Dean March's voice in such an intimate situation made Penny want to giggle like a schoolchild who just caught a teacher in a compromising position.

"Well?" Crenel sounded impatient.

"Werewolf," Penny blurted. "We found a werewolf. And there's an altar. Someone was here." She knew that her words weren't making a great deal of sense, but she couldn't seem to string a sentence together to save a life.

"I have your coordinates. I'll have a team there as soon as I can." Crenel ended the call before Penny could clarify that the werewolf was already dead and that whoever had summoned it had vanished.

"He couldn't have held on the line for one more minute?" Amelia muttered. "What are we supposed to do? Just hang around until backup arrives?"

"Apparently." Penny stared at her phone. "Wait a minute. Coordinates?"

"It's the FBI," Cisco said dryly. "They have *everyone's* coordinates."

Penny's phone vibrated in her hand, startling her into dropping it. She fished it back out of the fallen leaves, brushed it off, and answered, "Here I was, thinking you'd abandoned the four of us in the dark. And the cold. Holy fuck, is it cold here." As the adrenaline had worn off, the cold had seeped back into her bones, making her teeth chatter.

"Abandon you?" Crenel barked through crackling static.

"My wife would have my balls for breakfast if I even thought about it."

Penny heard the tsk of the irritated dean nearby. "So, do you always track our location?" she asked, not bothering to hide her irritation.

Crenel laughed. "Of course, I do. There's a team on their way. Now, find some damn cell reception and call me back so you can tell me exactly what happened."

CHAPTER EIGHT

Penny couldn't deny feeling a sense of relief when the team Crenel sent arrived in five shiny black SUVs instead of a helicopter.

Apart from the wind and the noise, she didn't want to draw attention to their little adventure if she could help it. Not that any of the partygoers back at the bonfire were sober enough to notice a Black Hawk landing in the middle of their party.

Agent Delouise led the operation, instructing the four biggest members of the team to secure the werewolf and load it into one of the cars. "You'll have to fold down the seats," she said. "Make sure you lay down some plastic. Carney will have my head if you get blood on the upholstery."

"We found this." Amelia held out the evidence bag. "By the altar. It's got blood on it."

Agent Delouise gingerly took it from her."You didn't touch it, did you?"

"I picked it up by the edges," Penny admitted. "But I didn't get any blood on my hands."

"Make sure you sanitize the hell out of yourself. I think I've got some rubbing alcohol in the car if you need it. Anything else?" The agent's eyes pierced into Penny's soul.

"No. Not really." She bit the inside of her cheek, wondering what exactly she could say.

"Bullshit."

Penny's eyebrows skyrocketed. "Excuse me?"

"Bullshit. There's something you're not telling me." Agent Delouise leaned closer to her. "Spill it."

Penny sidestepped. "There's nothing, really. Just... I dunno. It feels like we're missing something."

Delouise narrowed her eyes, then jerked her head down in a nod. "Trust your gut. I'll have my guys go over this whole place with a fine toothcomb—twice. As soon as your gut starts talking to your brain, let me know."

Relief washed through Penny. She could trust these Agents, she knew she could. They had the training that she didn't, and equipment to boot. Whatever was going on at that creepy makeshift altar, they were sure to figure it out.

"Thanks," she said. "Will you tell us if you find anything?"

The agent winked. "Depends if they let me."

Penny couldn't argue with that. "You need us for anything else?" she asked.

"You can go. Keep your phone on you, though."

With a grateful grin, Penny said goodbye, then she and her friends trudged back toward the road.

"Where's Boots?" Amelia whispered. "I'm guessing you already know. It's not like you'd leave her behind."

With a tired sigh, Penny jerked her thumb sideways. "I think she was trying to avoid all the fuss back there. She was hiding up a tree."

"Aww, the poor thing was scared?" Amelia crooned.

Penny snorted. "The 'poor thing' was hanging off a branch, making faces behind Delouise's back."

"Oh." Amelia darted a glance into the bushes. "Yeah, that does sound like Boots."

By the time they made it back to the bonfire, sleepy students were scattered around the dying fire. A guy strummed the guitar while he chatted with a pretty girl wrapped in a blanket, and a couple slow-danced nearby.

"I'm bushed." Penny sank down into the spot she had claimed earlier. She kicked off her shoes, unzipped her sleeping bag, and tucked her feet in, sandy socks and all.

Boots darted in beside her, wriggled around, and poked her nose out the top.

Within minutes, the gentle music had lulled Penny to sleep.

Crenel sat behind his tiny desk in his office at the Academy. One finger tapped the polished wood, a steady and unbroken rhythm that clawed at Penny's brain like nails down the chalkboard. "I know I don't have anything to go on," she protested. "But isn't your number one rule 'trust your gut?'"

"No, it's 'trust your team.' And my *team* tells me they didn't find anything." Finally, Crenel leaned back in his seat and ceased the infernal tapping. "Delouise said they scoured down to the bones. She's a good agent, and I trust her to do the job right. What would you have me do?"

Penny opened her mouth to answer but stopped. She growled, "I don't know," she admitted. "You're the expert, so think of something!"

"I *have* thought of something," Crenel said dryly. "Closing the case. We caught the werewolf. The wounds on the victims we've found so far are likely consistent with a werewolf attack."

Penny threw her hands up. "Okay. How many werewolf attacks have you seen?"

"No less than you had a few days ago," he pointed out. "Look, I know this is new. I know there's no precedent, there aren't any records we can match wounds and bite marks to. The guy we found had no DNA, and neither did the mess on that piece of linen."

"*No* DNA?" That made Penny pause.

Crenel sighed patiently. "You haven't gone over that in class yet? Mythers don't have any. Nothing, nada, blank slate. Makes it easy to tell one from a human or animal, but it's a bastard when we need to compare one to the other."

Penny's brain struggled with the reality of that. "Is that even possible?"

"Possible?" Crenel shrugged. "It's real. Think about it, kid. These creatures are made from human belief. Most of them were created in a time when they thought the common cold was caused by too much snot in your blood. Medicine was basically a bag of leeches and a hit of cocaine. You think those people considered the nuclear basis of their myths?" He shook his head bemusedly.

Penny's cheeks flushed. *Of course, he's right. I should have been able to figure that out myself.* "Look, all that proves is that the werewolf and the blood were both from Mythers," Penny pointed out.

Crenel shrugged. "I'll be the first to admit it's a guess, but it's our best guess, and the evidence that we found supports it." He placed both hands flat on his desk. "I know you're frustrated, and I know that there's a lot out there that we don't understand yet. But that doesn't mean everything has to have an extra layer to it. Sometimes, you just find the bad guy."

"It's not just that it was too easy," Penny protested. "What about the altar? Someone was there."

"Could have been the wolf. Maybe he did it before the moon came out." He held up a hand to forestall Penny's next question. "We looked, we really did. Delouise ran the plates of every car in that lot. All of them matched the beachgoers, and all of them agreed that no one went missing for long without an alibi. A couple of people mentioned an itinerant in the area, but their description matched our perp."

"There *is* something else. Something I can't put my finger on." Penny scowled, her frustration directed more at herself than the agent before her.

"That brings me back to my question, what the fuck do you want me to do about it?" Crenel asked. Irritation was showing in his voice now, the harsh scratch that tugged Penny's confidence down a notch. If nothing else, the agent had been incredibly patient with her.

"Fine." Penny threw herself out of the chair and toward

the door. "I'll drop it. But promise me...*promise* me that if anyone else is attacked, you'll send a team up there to investigate again."

"I promise." Crenel waited until she had yanked the door open before speaking again. "Penny, you'll make a good agent one day. You do have to trust your gut, to a degree. You also have to accept that sometimes, we're looking for an answer that doesn't exist."

Penny shut the door behind her without responding.

She stalked down the hallway, fists clenched and cheeks hot. *Why can't I let this go? I have nothing to go on.*

If only she could put her finger on what was bothering her.

If she had something concrete to go to Agent Crenel with, she had absolutely no doubt that he would listen. Until then, without some kind of evidence, she couldn't justify the manpower to him, and that meant he couldn't justify it to his superiors. She knew that, so why couldn't she let go of the itch at the back of her brain?

Penny drew in a deep breath and held it for a count of five. When she was done, she let it out in a slow hiss. She pulled the trigger.

Ping!

Through the scope, a black hole appeared in the middle of her target.

Ping! Ping! Two more shots, and two more holes mere inches away from the first.

"You're good," a voice said behind her.

Startled, Penny's trigger finger convulsively pulled back on the trigger, releasing her final round. The shot didn't even hit the target.

"When you're concentrating, anyway." Quaid patted her shoulder. "You need to learn how to focus under stress."

"Easy for you to say," Penny muttered. She engaged the safety and set the gun down on the table in front of her.

"Weapons down!" Quaid yelled.

"Down!" Penny called.

Quaid waited until the other three shooters lined up had confirmed before sending them to collect their targets.

Each student quickly totaled up their points. Thankful that their worst rounds didn't count—the round where Penny had received a big fat zero—she handed her slip into the teacher.

She stepped to the back room to join the rest of the waiting students.

"Amelia, Mara, Clive... Who've I missed?" Quaid squinted at the list of names in front of him.

"That's everyone, Professor," Mara confirmed. She grinned at Penny on the way past. "What score do we have to beat?"

A smirk twitched at Quaid's lips. "Perfect thirty."

Groaning, Mara stalked toward the shooting range.

Penny collapsed into a plastic chair. Across from her, Cisco gave her a hesitant grin.

"You okay, Penny?" he asked.

"Of course, I am," she snapped. She winced. "Sorry. Maybe. It's just, something is still bugging me."

Cisco didn't respond. They had been over it a hundred times already, much to Penny's growing frustration.

She knew if she couldn't even convince Cisco that something else was lurking out near the beach, she had no hope of convincing anyone else.

Eventually, she slumped. "It's not just that," she admitted. "I'm such a klutz. I dropped a whole magazine that night. Maybe if I'd reloaded my weapon faster, things would have gone more smoothly."

"It wasn't just you out there, remember." Cisco quickly swapped seats so that he was sitting next to her. He lowered his voice. "Look, three of us got rounds into that bastard. Amelia did a bang-up job of distracting it. No one got killed, and that's a good thing, right?"

"We might not be so lucky next time," Penny insisted. "What if I really cock-up? What if someone gets hurt because I dropped the ball?"

"Then train harder," Cisco said, shrugging. "Look, we all know you can shoot. You're top of the class. You just need to practice getting the bullets into the guns. It's a skill – like everything else. Just practice."

"Just practice!" Penny muttered. She ducked her head away from Cisco's skeptical gaze. "Fine. You've got a point, I guess. Practice."

With a satisfied smile, Cisco leaned back in his chair and crossed his arms. "How about you repay my invaluable advice with a coffee," he suggested.

It had become their ritual to escape to the local coffee shop every Monday afternoon, just the two of them, while Amelia took psychology, and Red waited for his afternoon research class.

It was the last thing Penny felt like doing. She looked at Cisco, knowing that his hopeful expression would drop into dismay if she refused. "Okay," she said at last. "But it's your turn to buy."

"Sure," Cisco agreed happily. "If you ask nicely, I'll even buy you cake."

CHAPTER NINE

Penny hunched further over her notebook as she scratched out three more job listings. She placed a pen on the next one, then her irritation bubbled over. She turned first to Boots, who hovered over her right shoulder, tongue flicking at Penny's ears, then to the left, where Cisco hovered.

"Can neither of you give a girl some space?" she snapped.

Cisco sank back into his chair, chagrined. "Sorry. Still having no luck with the job hunt?"

Penny shook her head. "I'm sorry too. I've been jumping around like a cat on a hot tin roof lately."

Cisco plucked the notebook out of her hands. "Well, here is your problem. You couldn't *pay* me enough to work at any of these places."

Penny gave him a wry smile. "I'm quickly coming to that realization. I've put in about forty applications, and the half-dozen interviews I've managed to get were all with complete idiots. Seriously, how are these people in charge of anything?"

The clink of china made Penny look up, and she gratefully accepted the coffee handed to her. "Thanks, Tony," she said.

Instead of returning to the machines, the barista snatched a chair from a nearby table and sat next to her.

"You're looking for a job?" Tony asked.

Penny shot a confused glance at Cisco. "Yeah. Why?"

"Do you know how to pull a coffee?"

Understanding dawned. Penny gave an apologetic shrug. "I only ever drank instant at home."

"Ugh, you poor thing. Never mind, you'll learn." He stuck a hand out for Penny to shake. "You're Penny, right? I own the cafe. Two of my girls quit last week, and my cook handed in his notice in this morning. Not because of me, I swear." He gave a nervous laugh. "Just… Portland's changed in the last few months, you know?" He glanced at Boots pointedly.

"Yeah," Penny agreed. She couldn't speak for Portland, but her own life had certainly turned upside down in the last six months.

"Well, half the people are bailing out to go somewhere a little quieter. At the same time, there is an influx of people looking for weird and wonderful things." Tony winked. "You can bring the snake to work with you. Who knows, maybe she could pull in a few customers of her own."

"But I just told you, I don't even know how to make a real coffee," Penny protested.

"It's not that hard," Cisco interjected. "You'll pick it up in no time. I mean, it can't be any harder than assembling a sniper rifle, right?"

A look of worry crossed Tony's face. "Uhh, right. What are you studying again?"

Hope thumped in Penny's chest. "I'm a fast learner," she assured Tony. "I work hard. I don't mind cleaning, and I'm really good at doing dishes."

He smiled. "Look, at the very least, come in for a trial. I'll show you how to use the machines, and you can get a feel for the place. When are you free?"

"What about Friday afternoon?" Penny suggested. "I've got an early class that finishes at eleven. Would that be okay?"

Tony nodded. "Sit tight. I'll grab your application form, and you can fill out your available times."

He sauntered back to the counter, pausing to take an order for a customer who hovered by the register.

"See?" Cisco said. "I told you it would work itself out."

"No, you didn't." Penny dumped a packet of sugar into her coffee and stirred it. "Wow. I finally made some progress on my job hunt, and now I'm crapping my pants."

"You'll do fine." Cisco laughed. "You'll have Boots there to help you. Do you know how to pull a coffee, Boots?"

Boots gave a cheerful hiss, then proceeded to dunk her entire face into Penny's drink.

"Ew! Boots, that's disgusting." Penny unfolded a paper napkin and held it out for Boots to rub her head on.

"She's just getting a taste for the merchandise," Cisco said. He picked up his own coffee—now cold, Penny was sure—and drizzled some of it on the saucer. Boots pushed herself along the tabletop and flicked her tongue in the dish.

"Not too much," Penny warned. "You won't be able to sleep tonight."

Boots lifted her head and looked Penny in the eye. She made a coughing sound from the back of her throat, one that Penny was sure signified a laugh.

"Fine, you don't sleep anyway. Smartass."

Penny eyed her coffee. Then, figuring she ate with the snake, slept with the snake, and occasionally got licked by the snake, decided a few more germs couldn't hurt. *Maybe Mythers are germ proof as well as DNA-free.* She took a sip.

"And you say *I'm* disgusting." Cisco punctuated his remark by wiping the cake crumbs from his mouth with his shirt.

"That's because you are," Penny said.

"Ha-ha." He leaned back and rested a hand on his bloated stomach. "I solved one of your big problems. What else can I help you with?"

"*You* solved it?" Penny asked in mock outrage. "That was all me, thank you very much."

"You wouldn't even be here if I hadn't insisted," he pointed out. "If I wasn't so annoying, you wouldn't have complained about it loud enough for Tony to hear."

Penny relented. "Fine. Maybe you helped…a little."

Penny crouched, waiting for Jason to strike. She tried to shut out the buzz in her mind, tried to focus.

I sent a team out, Crenel had told her earlier. *We scoured the area. There was nothing.*

Jason lunged. Penny blocked, but clumsily. Her foot snapped up and kicked his hip, and he spun away.

Sometimes your gut's just wrong.

A fist flew past her face, missing by inches.

Sometimes your gut's just wrong.

Jason shifted. Penny's instincts warred. Was it a feint? She twisted to block a blow that never came. Instead, an elbow connected with her cheekbone. Pain blossomed across her face, and she cried out.

"Oh, shit. Sorry." Jason pulled back immediately as Penny fell to her knees, clutching her face. "I didn't think you'd actually *fall* for that."

Glass knelt in front of Penny, his eyes hard and unsympathetic. "Hingston! You weren't paying attention."

"Yes, I was!" Penny winced as the words pulled at her sore cheek. Above the swelling bruise, her eye throbbed. "I saw him move, so I blocked it."

"You didn't trust your gut." Glass's words, coming so soon on the heels of Crenel's lecture, knocked the wind out of Penny.

"My face hurts." Penny knew the words were unneeded. Even the grouchy professor's face was now creased with worry as he gently prodded her cheekbone.

"Non-contact sparring for the rest of class. You can go at eleven," Glass barked. The instructions made little sense to Penny until he helped her to her feet. "I'll walk you to the first aid office."

Oh. She must be hurt badly if he was offering a personal escort.

Glass said little as they traipsed through the academy halls, Penny's hand cupped on her face as she leaned against him. Her head spun from the blow, and darkness had clouded her vision on one side.

They passed through the foyer just as three special agents in crisp suits and dark glasses strode out of the building. When the door *thunked* shut behind them, Glass spoke.

"Rumor has it you're going toe to toe with the liaison." He released his grip on Penny to lean forward and open a door, then looped her arm over his shoulder. "Something about a werewolf?"

"I had a hunch. He checked it out," Penny said, careful to speak without moving her jaw or lips. Though the words came out muffled, Glass seemed to understand.

"And?" he prodded.

Penny shrugged. "I was wrong."

"Were you really?" He leaned her against a wall, letting it prop her up while he fished out a set of keys and unlocked the door to the first aid room. "I find that hard to believe. You've got good instincts, Hingston." He eyed her cheek. "Usually."

Penny stumbled forward. "Doesn't matter what anyone believes," she said. "He checked it out." Her eyes rolled back as she collapsed into a chair, willing the blinding pain to ease.

"Then you *don't* believe it," Glass persisted.

Something cold and hard prodded Penny's cheek, sending a fresh surge of pain into her skull. Before she could react, a wave of frozen sparks took her breath away. Then the pain was gone.

Penny blinked, forcing her eyes to focus on the object waving in front of her.

Glass held the Asclepius staff in one hand while he filled out the requisition form with the other. "What's your first name again, Hingston?"

"It's Penny." She answered the list of questions he rattled off: her date of birth (twenty-two years and a few months ago), known allergies (none), medical history (boringly healthy).

He shoved the form at her to sign. "Eat within the next twenty minutes, and avoid further use of the staff for the next three days, except in emergencies."

Next, Glass rattled off the list of instructions attached to a tag dangling from the staff's snake head. "Students should be aware that overuse of the staff may cause confusion, starvation, lethargy, and death. Staff is restricted for use on life-threatening injuries or injuries that present the possibility of permanent damage. Use on broken bones may cause permanent malformation, and is not recommended except in the direst of circumstances."

He narrowed his eyes. "Huh. I hope it wasn't broken. I probably should have read the warnings first." He shrugged and turned to put the staff away. "That whack to the head would constitute life-threatening, anyway. Your eye looked like it was about to pop out of your head."

"Gee, thanks," Penny said dryly. "I could have lived without *that* image, you know."

"Better to be aware of what your bad choices could have caused," Glass said without a hint of humor.

"I blocked," Penny insisted.

Glass stepped up to her, face stern, posture intimidating. "Your gut is never wrong, Hingston. Learn to trust it before it gets you killed."

CHAPTER TEN

Penny touched her healed cheekbone before walking into the bustling coffee shop. *Thank God for that staff.* Starting her one-day trial with a huge purple bruise on her face wouldn't have been good.

Inside, three people were queued at the register, which was manned by a girl with violet hair and a nose ring. Two more waited for their orders, and a quick glance showed Penny three tables with numbers and no food. *Damn. He had to start me on a day like this?*

"Hey! You're here!" Tony waved her over and pointed to a door behind the counter with one hand, frothing a jug of milk with the other. "Throw your stuff out back, and let's get started!"

Penny did as directed, pushing through the swinging door to find a small staff room equipped with a sink, kettle, and shelves. Two black aprons hung on hooks by the door, and a small table took up one corner. She slipped her handbag next to a purple tote—it matched the color of the server's hair, so Penny guessed it was hers—and set Boots' bag on the floor. "Why don't you stay out here for a bit, pet?"

Boots sniffed the air and looked around disdainfully. The room was plain and cold, and the two chairs tucked under the table were made of hard plastic. Penny realized the snake wouldn't be at all comfortable stuck in here for her four-hour shift.

"Fine. Just stay out of the way, okay? I don't want you to get hurt if it gets any busier out there." Penny grabbed an apron and slipped it over her head, and pushed the door open.

The smell of coffee and a buzz of chatter hit her like a wall. She took a deep breath and walked over to Tony.

"Looks like you're set," he said with a grin. He passed a coffee to a waiting man and began another. "Oh, Snakey came too!" Tony pointed to a small basket in the corner. "I've set you up a little hidey-hole over there, beautiful. I'll bring you some chocolate milk soon, okay?"

Boots twitched her tail happily and scooted over to the basket.

"You're sure it's okay?" Penny asked.

"Sure." Tony jerked his head toward the snuggling serpent. "She's not an animal, more like a person. Like that little green guy that walked past the other day. She's one of *them*."

"She is," Penny admitted. "But not everyone likes...*them*. Most people will think she's just a normal snake." She didn't add that she was surprised Tony could see Boots for what she was, let alone a passing leprechaun.

"Anyone who doesn't like it can get the hell out of my shop." He grinned and slid another coffee over the counter.

"But hey, it's Portland. She'll be our main attraction before long, just you wait and see."

Penny wasn't sure how to respond to that. She didn't relish the idea of Boots being turned into the star of a freak show, but perhaps Tony was just trying to make them comfortable. She was saved from responding, however.

"Tony!" The purple-haired girl flicked a tea towel at him and passed over a long receipt. "Man, pay attention. I just got an order for three vanilla caps and a macchiato. Get with it!"

"Do you want me to clear those tables first?" she asked.

Tony gave a grateful nod. "Bart will show you where to put them."

Bart? Shrugging it off, Penny scooted out to gather the scattered cups and plates left by diners. She stacked them as high as she felt comfortable—which wasn't very—and made her way to the kitchen.

"Hey, new girl!" The chef waved her down. "Throw those in there." He gestured to a big industrial dishwasher.

Penny followed his instructions, slotting the plates and cups in as he directed. "You must be Bart," she guessed.

"The one and only. Can you shoot that out to number thirteen?" He thrust a tray at her, two plates with toasted sandwiches and a side of fries.

"Sure." Penny rested the tray on one arm and awkwardly pushed the kitchen door open.

"Hit it with your ass," Bart called.

Startled, Penny almost upset her tray.

"Go through the door backward," Bart clarified. "So you don't drop anything."

"Oh!" Penny grinned and swung her hip to shove the door open. "That's easier."

She delivered the tray, and on her way back to the kitchen, Tony snagged her.

"Here," he said. "Can you hold this?" He grabbed her hand and wrapped it around the handle of a bubbling jug of milk. "Just keep the nozzle about…yep, there."

He darted off to throw lids on two waiting coffees and hand them to an impatient woman nearby.

"About time," she snapped. "What took you so long?"

"It was all the love I put in the cups." Tony smiled sweetly, but although it made Penny laugh, the woman didn't seem to be mollified.

"Heathen boy. Tell Bart his lasagna was wonderful yesterday." She walked out, shoulders still set with righteous irritation despite the small smile tugging at the corners of her mouth. "Violet, dear. Don't you let that horrible man boss you around too much!"

"I won't, Mrs. B. Catch you tomorrow!" Violet waved with one hand while the other punched a new order into the register.

Penny's milk was bubbling and foaming almost to the top of the jug when Tony rescued her.

He eyed the pot. "Damn." He spun and tossed it down a nearby sink, then poured a fresh batch. "Maybe stick with the tables for now. I'll show you how to make the world's best coffee when it gets a bit quieter, okay?"

Relieved to have something to do she felt capable of, Penny nodded. She grabbed an empty tray and started loading it with plates.

A well-dressed woman wearing too much jewelry and

enough perfume to choke an elephant grabbed her wrist. "Here. Take this. You're too slow, girl, so don't expect a tip."

"I don't?" Penny blushed, realizing this was a customer, and she was here to get a job. "I'm sorry. I'm just here on a trial. It's my first day. I'm sure I'll get faster."

"You can't train stupid." The woman turned back to her coffee with a sneer.

Penny hurriedly took her empty plates and stacked them on her tray.

"Nasty old cow," Penny muttered under her breath. As if sensing her discomfort, Boots peeked out from her basket. Penny set her tray down on an empty table and ducked down to give her a scratch. "It's okay, mate. You go back to sleep." She stood and picked the tray back up.

"*What is that?*"

Penny swung around, only to find the asshole woman who'd snarked at her staring Boots down.

Boots raised her head and hissed at the woman

"It's one of...of those *things*, isn't it? No normal animal would show that sort of aggression." Spittle flew from the woman's mouth as she ranted.

The rest of the shop had fallen quiet.

"You've got demons here! I won't abide it. Those things will bring about the end of the world!" She shoved a finger toward Penny's face. "And you! You're friends with it, so you're probably one yourself!"

The woman shoved Penny's arm, sending her staggering back in shock. Plates slid to the ground, shattering in a cascade of tinkling crashes.

Penny crouched among the wreckage, fists clenched and shaking. *You can't hit her back. You can't.* Her instincts, always on the defensive side, urged her otherwise, but she clamped down on her rage, swallowing it like a lumpy, bitter ball. She looked around, floundering in a situation she couldn't control.

"See!" The woman turned to her audience, proud. "She's cursed! This…this *witch* touched my food. I want my money back! I'm not eating in a place that curses its patrons!"

"Get the hell out of my shop." Breaking the spell, Tony strode over and grabbed the woman's arm. "Get out before I call the cops and press assault charges."

"Assault?" the woman yelled. She tried to pull away, but his grip was tight. "You've got your hands on me. That's assault! *Assault!*" She screamed the word dramatically, eyes wide as she looked for support among the small number of customers waiting nearby. Each stepped back, unwilling to stand up for the woman.

"You assaulted my worker," Tony spat. "Now get the fuck out of here before you make it worse for yourself." He steered her for the door. "Don't come back here again."

Seeing the woman retreat brought Penny back to the moment. The adrenaline fled from her body, and she sank to the ground. Hands trembling, she began to stack the broken china onto the tray, and she blinked away the traitorous sting in her eyes.

"Jesus." Tony bent down and grabbed her hand. Penny flinched backward. "Go take a break. That woman won't be coming back."

"No, I'm—" A jagged edge sliced Penny's hand, and she groaned. "Shit. Okay." She lifted her eyes to meet her would-be employer's. "Sorry, Tony."

"Hey, you didn't make her a bitch." He clapped her shoulder reassuringly and steered her toward a free table.

Behind him, Violet swept up the mess with a dustpan and broom.

Penny sank onto the chair, clutching a paper napkin to her cut. She'd waved off Tony's attention, assuring him she'd be fine. She would be; it wasn't too deep, and the blood would stop flowing soon, surely.

Something soft nudged her ankle, then wrapped around it, climbing up to the table.

"Hey, girl." Penny dropped her head so Boots could lick her cheek. "It's not so bad. Just give me a minute and—"

"Hey." Tony pulled a chair out and sat beside her. "Let me see that hand."

Penny let him examine it. "It doesn't hurt too much. If I can wrap it up, I can—"

"Don't you even say it." Tony let go and sighed. "It's gonna need stitches. I can drive you to a clinic or get Violet to do it. Her shift is over soon anyway."

"No!" Penny waved off the offer of help. "There's a nurse at the Academy. It's fine, really." Her shoulder slumped as reality hit. "I guess my trial's over?"

"You can't make coffee like that. Unless it's for a vampire..." He leaned closer. "Are vampires real? I keep seeing new reports from New York."

Penny nodded, a smile finally growing. "Yeah, but you don't wanna mess with those."

"Look, we'll call an end to today. I think you're well and truly ready to go home. But come back Monday, and we'll talk about your roster, okay?"

Disbelief fell away to shock, then excitement. "Really? You're still giving me the job?"

"Yeah." Tony grinned. "You did great."

"He's just glad he found someone who doesn't whine about clearing tables." Violet slid a coffee in front of Penny. "Here. You look like you need this."

"Thanks." Penny dropped her eyes so Violet wouldn't see them glitter. *What the hell, Penny? You're not a crier!* The day had exhausted her, though, first with the anxiety and excitement of something new, then the rush of being attacked in a way she hadn't expected. All her training had focused on how to fight back with fists and weapons, how to hurt and disable her opponent. None of it had covered what to do in a situation like that.

I suppose I'm just lucky I didn't do anything that could get me arrested. She wasn't sure if the Academy would have been able to bail her out for hurting a civilian. The last thing she needed was a record or worse, to be deported.

Tony and Violet let her be, returning to the job of running the busy coffee shop. Bart came out once to check on her and once to offer her a meal, but easily accepted her claim that she wasn't hungry. Penny just wanted to finish her coffee and be alone.

CHAPTER ELEVEN

"Thank you, Tony. No, really, don't apologize. I completely understand. You, too. Bye." Penny clicked the end call button on her phone and took a deep, steadying breath. Then, she pegged it across the dining hall. It bounced off a table and onto the floor, and Penny immediately winced. *I know the case said shock-proof, but that might have been a little much.*

"Hey!" One of the guys from the new intake sat up in shock. "That nearly hit me!"

"It was nine feet away!" Penny growled back. She slid deeper into her chair, scowling.

"Penny?" Amelia said gently. "You wanna talk about it?"

"No," Penny huffed. It was a lie. "She called the health department! Can you believe it? Of all the scummy, bullshit things to do, and they *believed* her! Now Tony has to close for a week, and I don't have a job. I swear, if I ever run into that horrible cow again, I'll—"

"Woah." Cisco grabbed Penny's arm firmly enough that

she realized her hands were clenched into fists. "Slow down. Who called the health department?"

"That nasty bigot, the one who called Boots a demon." She'd told her friends about the horrendous job trial two days ago.

"Yikes." Cisco pulled back to give Penny her space. "So, um. Does that mean you didn't get the job after all?"

Penny nodded, not quite trusting her voice.

"We should hunt her down," Red growled. Penny's head jerked up to look at him. "Rip her throat out." His eyes glittered darkly but cleared when he shook his head and grinned. Red gave a nervous laugh.

"What the fuck is wrong with you?" Amelia asked. Her tone was light, but a worried frown creased her brow. "You've been off for days. Your skin is hot. Do you have a fever?" She pressed the back of her hand to his cheek.

Red gave a nervous laugh and brushed her away. "I told you, I'm fine. I just need a decent night's sleep."

"Are you still having the dreams?" Amelia pressed.

"What dreams?" Penny looked from one to the other. "Is something going on, Red?"

"No!" Red brushed the question off. "I've just had a few restless nights, that's all. I'll be right as rain in no time."

"Restless doesn't begin to describe it," Cisco muttered in Penny's ear. "Last night, he was yapping like a dog in his sleep."

He'd spoken quietly, but not quietly enough to evade Red's hearing. The Irishman glowered at his friend. "Maybe I should let out whose name you were moaning in your sleep the other night?"

Cisco hastily shut that idea down, his face turning so

red it was almost purple. "It was a joke, man. Just a joke. Here, I'll take your plate back up to the kitchen. Do you want anything else to eat?"

In response, Red's stomach growled. "I'm starving. Another burger?"

Penny's eyes bugged out. "Red, you just ate a burger, fries, coleslaw, two roast potatoes, *and* Amelia's leftovers."

Red frowned. "You're right." He looked over his shoulder to call to Cisco. "Get me some roast potatoes, too!"

Amelia shook her head. "You're gonna get so fat."

Red patted his stomach. "A big lad needs a big feed to keep his energy up. Speaking of energy, what are we doing tonight?"

"Tonight?" Penny shook her head. "I'm going for a long shower and an early bed."

"No way." Amelia grabbed her hand. "You need a break. Come on, let's go out. We need to blow off some steam, especially you. Who knows? Maybe a night out will lift your spirits and change your luck."

Penny shuddered. The last thing she wanted to do was go out in public. She'd much rather spend the night curled up under a blanket, alone and miserable. She dropped her head into her hands. "What happened to me? I've turned into a miserable old lady!"

Amelia clapped delightedly. "That's my girl! Come on, we'll have a blast."

"Who's having a blast?" Cisco slid Red's packed plate in front of him.

"We're going out," Red said, his voice already muffled with a mouthful of food.

"You're such an animal," Amelia said with a note of disgust in her voice.

"Aye, I am." Red burped proudly. "You know you love it."

"I love it like a hole in the head," Amelia said. She stood and grabbed Penny's empty plate, stacking it on top of her own. "Come on, Penn. Let's leave these disgusting boys to gorge. We can go upstairs and play with each other's hair."

"Can I watch?" Red called.

"You're disgusting," Amelia yelled over her shoulder. As they walked away, her smile faded quickly.

"Amelia, are you sure he's okay?" Red didn't seem terribly off to her. He'd always been a little exuberant, though the last few days he'd been taking it a little far even for him. It was Amelia's reaction that was worrying her.

"Did you see the bags under his eyes?" Amelia asked. "I don't think he's slept at all in the last two days. It's making him really cranky, and...well, really *weird*."

"How so?" Penny asked. They reached their room and Penny unlocked the door, holding it open for Amelia.

Inside, Amelia pushed up the sleeve of her shirt. A circular bruise on her forearm was just starting to show tinges of yellow around the blue and purple edges.

Penny leaned in for a better look. "Amelia, did he hit you?"

Amelia yanked the sleeve back down. "He didn't mean to hurt me. We were just mucking around, you know? He was licking my wrist, and then—"

"Licking your wrist?" Penny couldn't hide a grin at that.

"There's nothing wrong with that, Penny." Amelia rolled her eyes. "Anyway, Clive walked up behind him and slapped his back. It gave him a real fright, and somehow, he bit me. I wasn't expecting it, and it hurt, the bastard."

The alarm bells ringing in Penny's ears were so loud she almost couldn't hear Amelia talk. "Amelia—"

Amelia shook her head. "I know what you're going to say. I told him it wasn't cool, and if he ever does anything like that again, he's dead. Dead and dumped." She sank down on her bed. "Come on. I'll straighten your hair for you."

Penny resisted the urge to argue. Amelia was head-strong and proud, but she could take care of herself, and if she couldn't? Penny would be right behind her, ready to have her back the moment she was needed.

Penny leaned her head back, feeling the gentle tug of the brush running through her hair.

"Any more job prospects lined up?" Amelia asked.

Penny shook her head, wincing when the movement yanked on a snarl in her hair. "Not a damned thing. I've got enough drinking money for the rest of the semester, but that's about it. Having that Jeep the other weekend really makes me want a car."

"That was a month ago. I can't believe the semester is passing so fast." Amelia tipped Penny's head forward and gathered her hair up in a clip, leaving a small section out at the back.

Penny could feel the heat of the straightener in the back of her neck, and a delicious shiver ran down her spine.

"A month?" Penny's mind brushed against the memory of stalking through the woods that night. Everything about it—the strange altar, the bloodied bandage, the mysterious scream that had set them on the hunt in the first place—still haunted her.

Amelia loosened another section of hair. "Now you're dwelling on it again, aren't you?"

"Guilty as charged." Penny fell silent, trying to concentrate on the tug and pull and sliding warmth at the back of her head. "Did you know Mythers don't have DNA?"

"As in, they don't match anything on record?" Comb, press, slide. Amelia had settled into a steady rhythm now.

"As in, they don't have any. Crenel said there was no way to match that blood to the body, or to anything else. Apparently, every Myther is the same!" In her frustration, Penny moved her head just as Amelia was pressing the straightener down on a section of hair. She sucked in a sharp breath as her scalp touched the iron.

"Stay still!" Amelia clicked her tongue. "You're going to end up with third-degree burns all over your head if you don't calm down."

"Sorry," Penny muttered.

"You know, it's not just Red that's out of sorts. You've been really jumpy." As she spoke, Amelia rose to her knees so she could work on the top layers of Penny's hair. "Look, I know that it's bugging you. There's nothing you can do about it, though. If something is still out there, eventually, someone will see it, and when they do, Crenel will realize you were right all along, and he'll spend the rest of the semester sucking eggs."

"I suppose." Penny picked at a loose thread on Amelia's comforter. "It's the not knowing that's frustrating me. No matter what he says, I can't seem to let this rest, and knowing that I was probably wrong, but not that I was *definitely* wrong seems to be throwing my head for a loop."

"You definitely need to get drunk," Amelia said flatly. "We all do. But no more beaches, for crying out loud. It's turned you and Red barking mad."

Penny could feel Amelia still behind her but thought nothing of it until the smell of singed hair tickled her nose. "Dude!" Penny jerked her head forward and the hair came free of the straighteners.

"Oh shit! I'm so sorry, Penny!" Amelia quickly examined the damaged hair. "It's not so bad, I promise."

Penny could deal with a bit of singed hair. It wasn't like the rest of it was under control on any given day. She was more concerned about what had made her friend drift off into space like that. "What happened?"

Amelia gave an unconvincing laugh. "Just a stupid thought. Like, a really, *really* dumb one."

Her tone of voice said something different, though. Something had occurred to Amelia—something she didn't want to admit.

Penny slid off the bed and turned to face her. "Spill."

Amelia waved it off, laughing again. "You'll just laugh. Which you should, because it's ridiculous. It's just, when I called you and Red barking mad..." She winced.

Penny's eyes widened. Then she laughed. "You think Red has turned into a *werewolf*?"

Seeming relieved that Penny thought the idea was ridiculous too, Amelia gave a more convincing giggle this time. "I know, it's ridiculous. He didn't even get bitten, just scratched, and it's not like he's gotten all hairy or anything like that. But when we were talking about the werewolf, I remembered what Cisco said about Red yapping in his sleep..." She gave an embarrassed shrug. "At least you had your entertainment for the day."

Penny leaned down to give her friend a hug. "He's *not* a werewolf," she said confidently. "We would absolutely know if he was."

Amelia pulled back with a look of bemusement. "Well, I *know* that," she said, laughing. "Now, what are you wearing? You can't dress down when your hair looks like that."

CHAPTER TWELVE

Penny ducked under the plastic awning just in time to avoid the fat drops of rain that had begun to fall.

"My hair!" She squealed, bursting through the doors and into the Chinese restaurant. "Is it wet?" She patted it down while Amelia assured her that, no, the weather hadn't made it explode into a giant frizzy halo.

"Damn!" Only a few seconds behind her, Cisco hadn't been so lucky. "It really opened up out there, didn't it?"

Penny ducked his soggy bear hug. "Touch my hair and you die," she threatened.

Cisco laughed. "Okay! I get the picture. Did you book a table?"

"Sure did." Penny didn't admit she'd used the online form to book said table while they were in the Uber, two streets away. "Let me go ask."

Cisco tailed her to the small kiosk where a young Chinese girl was furiously writing notes. She looked up when Penny approached, startled. A quick peek showed that rather than bookings, she'd been working through an advanced chemistry textbook.

"Hi. I booked a table for Hingston?" Penny gave the girl a winning smile. When the attendant blushed, scrambling to find the reservation, Penny added, "I used the online form. It hasn't been long. Maybe it didn't go through?"

The girl tapped a screen in front of her. "Oh! I see it. Here, you can sit at table nineteen. It's a lucky number, you know."

"Really? I could do with some luck."

Amelia leaned in close to whisper in Penny's ear. "I've come here a few times. According to the staff, every table number is lucky."

Penny groaned. "You could have let me believe it anyway."

The waitress scurried away to get menus while Cisco, Amelia, and Penny sat. Amelia craned her neck to look at the door.

As she did, it blew open again to let Red in, along with a stiff breeze and a scatter of leaves. "Blow me down, it's as windy as a box of farts out there!" He shoved the door shut and gave a toothy grin. "Who's buying?"

"I am," Cisco said, surprising Penny. He winked. "If I'm going to offer, it'll be here, not at a bar full of top-shelf whiskey."

Red's face stilled and he sucked in a long breath, nostrils flaring. "What's that smell" His eyes darted to a corner of the shop.

Something moved in the corner. Penny tensed, ready to flee if it was a rat. Instead, the creature—she thought it was a cat—uncurled and stalked toward the Irishman, its golden fur reflecting the light from the paper lanterns hanging from the ceiling.

The cat sat at Red's feet and hissed. Red tensed, his neck muscles tight and his hands clenched. The waitress looked up from her textbook and hurried over.

"Maneki-neko! Bad cat. You are here to bring the customers in, not scare them away." She picked up the golden feline and waved Red through. "I'm sorry. She won't hurt you."

"It's not the cat I'm worried about," Red growled. He walked to the table, his stride smooth but somehow unsettling.

"Woah." Amelia put her hand on his arm and pulled him down to sit next to her. "You okay?"

"Just hungry." Red flashed another grin and snatched up a menu. "I'll have the potstickers, some honey-fried wings, the kung-pao beef, and…maybe the pork belly rice."

Penny waited for Red to laugh. When he simply continued to flick through the menu, she glanced at Amelia. Her friend's eyes were narrowed.

"I take it back," Cisco said. "I'm too broke to feed this giant."

"Red, you ate two whole plates of food at lunch today," Amelia said. "What is going on?"

"I'm a growing lad?" Red seemed genuinely confused by his friends' reactions. "Seriously. I'm starving!"

Thunder boomed, making Penny jump. "Well, I might have the chow mein." She glanced longingly at the bar. "Anyone else want a drink?"

"Whiskey!" Red called.

"Margaritas?" Amelia suggested.

Glad the tension had eased, Penny went to order their drinks. By the time she returned with a margarita pitcher, a whiskey poured from a dusty bottle on the bottom shelf, and a beer, her friends were chatting happily with the waitress, who'd arrived to take their order.

To Penny's shock, Red ordered everything he'd asked for, as well as a round of spring rolls. "To share," he insisted, although the way he licked his lips suggested that might not be the case.

As the waitress walked away, Penny saw Red slip Cisco three twenties with an apologetic smile. Cisco attempted to refuse, but Red shoved them back.

The food came quickly, and it was good. Penny dove into her dish, soon regretting the two spring rolls Red had shared with her. Halfway through, she sat back and rubbed her stomach.

"I'm so full," Penny moaned.

"You're not finishing that?" Red asked, his eyes on her half-eaten dish.

Penny blinked. "Red? You did *not* eat all that food."

He blushed and shrugged. "I told you, growing."

Penny sighed. "Sure, go for it. But can you go fetch us another jug?" She held up the empty pitcher and dug in her handbag for her purse.

Pain stung her wrist. She looked down to see the golden cat lean back on his haunches, then pounce on the table. It hissed at Red.

His eyes narrowed. "I told you, cat. I'm hungry."

The cat hissed again and lifted a paw toward the door.

"Kitty really doesn't like you, babe." Amelia's voice held

a hint of worry. She glanced at Penny, teeth tugging her lip. "Why is that?"

Silence fell. Penny realized that the rain had stopped.

"Guys? We're pretty much done. Maybe we could ask for a doggy bag..." Electricity buzzed in the air, making Penny's hair stand on end. *Just the storm,* she told herself. *Residual electricity. That's all.*

"Good idea." Cisco's voice was grim. "Red, I'll sort out the bill. Maybe you should wait outside before this cat tries to tear strips off you."

Rubbing her stinging wrist, Penny nodded. "I'll walk you out." She snatched up her handbag, and the cat let out a comfortable purr.

"We're gonna let this bag of fleas—" Red backed down when the cat hissed again, rising up on its back legs. "Okay. Guess we are." He glanced back at Penny's plate. "Make sure they pack that up, though. I'm *not* leaving good food behind just because Mr. Whiskers here doesn't like me."

Penny hurried to the exit, doing her best to ignore the fingers running chills down her spine.

"Hey!" Cisco grabbed her arm. "Are you guys gonna be okay out there while I settle the bill?"

Despite a frisson of worry at his words, Penny nodded. "Of course. Red's fine. He's just....hungry?"

Red burst out into the cool air and Penny followed, darting forward when he staggered.

"Penny?" He looked up, his eyes wild. "Penny, I don't feel so good."

"Was it the chicken?" As soon as she said it, she felt like an idiot. This wasn't bad food. It was something else.

"Snap out of it," Amelia said briskly. She grabbed his

arm and yanked him upright. "I don't know what's going on with you, Red, but we're going back to the Academy, and we're going to *deal* with it."

The streetlight flickered. Penny glanced up as the moon began to peek out from behind a fleeing storm cloud. "We should get you home," she said.

Red snarled. His lips pulled back to bare his white teeth.

Penny's eyes widened. *I never realized how pointed they are.* The thought passed in an instant, lost in panic when Red hunched over, his body contorting as he growled in pain.

"Red!" Amelia screamed as Cisco burst through the door, grabbing his friend just before he collapsed into the muddy gutter.

"Stay with me, buddy!" Cisco called.

Red shoved him back, and Cisco went flying. Standing, Red gave a furious roar as his face…*stretched*. His mouth elongated, his whiskery beard turning to fur as he fell back to all fours. His shredded clothes fell away to reveal the enormous wolf he had turned into.

"Penny? Penny, what do we do?"

Amelia's sobs tore at Penny's heart, even as a howl drowned them out.

Red, now a five-foot-tall, shaggy red wolf, bounded down the street away from them.

Penny watched him go with her heart sinking in her chest. "I don't know, mate. I don't know."

Penny, Cisco, and Amelia reluctantly trudged back into the Academy not long after daybreak the next morning.

Penny pushed the door open first and slumped when she saw Dean March standing in the middle of the foyer, arms folded. "Morning, Dean."

A crawl of discomfort made its way up Penny's spine, even though she technically hadn't done anything wrong.

While the Academy didn't have a curfew, turning up to class after spending all night on the town—or hunting a werewolf—wasn't endorsed. However, the dean had long since admitted that there wasn't a damn thing she could do to stop them as long as their grades didn't suffer.

The dean sighed. "I've been waiting for you three to return. Come with me."

Shooting Amelia and Cisco a worried glance, Penny trailed after the Academy's head.

Instead of taking them to her office, the dean led them down the corridor, past the small storerooms, and into the infirmary, a single-bed bay that was used for students who were sick or injured.

Lying on that bed, blanket tucked up to his chin and dirt smeared on his face, was Red.

"I don't know whether to kiss him or slap him," Amelia whispered.

Penny giggled, her relief and exhaustion welling into tears. "Thank god he's okay. Now I'm going to *kill* him."

Red twitched and opened an eye. "Come on, now. I thought you'd be a wee bit more excited than that."

"You stupid, stupid man," Amelia said, voice rising as she ranted. "I *told* you to get that scratch checked. I *told* you that you were acting strange. Barking in your sleep?

Fevers, mood swings, and do you *know* how much you've been eating lately? Why didn't you *listen*? Instead, you go and harass a poor cat, ruin your best shirt, and keep us out all night looking for you while you were here all along!"

Voice cracking at the end, Amelia sank down on her knees next to the bed. "I'm so glad you're okay," she whispered.

"He turned up at the Academy entrance just after dawn," the dean explained crisply. "Naked."

"I did?" Red asked, wincing. "I don't remember that bit." He peeked under his blanket and blushed a fiery pink. "Oh, bollocks."

Cisco snorted, covering it with a cough. "I'm glad you were able to get him into bed, Dean March." Then, realizing what he said, he clapped a hand over his face. "I didn't mean—"

"I enlisted Professor Glass' and Professor Craster's assistance." Dean March allowed herself a small smirk. "Thankfully, no students were present at the time."

"Small favors, I guess." Red shuffled to sit up, careful to keep the blanket covering everything from his chest down. "Can I get some clothes? How long until class?"

"You'll be excused for the day," March said. "As will your friends. They will need to speak to our research team." A refined eyebrow twitched. "You do realize that you are the first live werewolf specimen we've had access to?"

"You're going to use me as a research project?" Red moaned. "Strike me down. I just want it fixed!"

"That may be easier said than done," the dean admitted. Seeing his face fall, she added, "But I'm sure it can be done.

It is simply a matter of sorting the variations of werewolf myths to identify the relevant cure."

"Aye. Simple." Red's tone suggested he didn't believe it for a minute.

"Perhaps." The dean stepped back toward the door. "Someone will be here shortly to make notes on the events that led up to your...condition. I'd suggest you find some clothes before then."

Red gave Cisco an anguished look. "Mate, could you please? I don't want some old lady poking and prodding my bits while I'm in my birthday suit."

A sly smile crept over Cisco's face. "What's it worth to you?"

"What?" Amelia socked him in the thigh. "Don't even joke about that."

"Ow." Cisco held his hands up to ward off another blow. "All right! I'll go get you some clothes. Just... don't wolf out while I'm gone."

"It's not a full moon, you fool," Red said in a withering tone. "Don't you know anything about werewolves?"

"No... but I know you're a natural redhead." Cisco ignored Red's outraged plea for an explanation, darting out of the infirmary and shutting the door behind him.

"What did he mean?" Red demanded. His eyes were locked on Amelia, suspiciously avoiding Penny.

"I can't imagine," Amelia said sweetly.

Red covered his face. "Don't tell me half of Portland has seen me tallywhacker now."

Penny couldn't help but laugh. "No, Red, it's ok. Well, I don't know who saw *what* when you came back, but *we* didn't see anything."

Red frowned. "Then what did he mean, a 'natural redhead?'"

"You turned into a wolf the color of a ginger tabby," Penny explained.

"Hmph." Red settled back under the blankets. "Well, at least we get a day off class."

"It's Monday," Penny reminded him. "Weapons is one of my favorite subjects!"

"Oh." His face fell, then brightened again with hope. "Did I at least teach that smarmy cat a lesson? I hope I stepped on its ugly tail. The wee prick was giving me the evil eye all through dinner."

"No," Amelia sighed. "And don't even think about going back there. That poor waitress saw everything, and she's probably checked herself into an institution by now."

"Actually, she seemed to take it pretty well," Penny admitted.

The girl had chased Cisco out with the handful of change he'd abandoned. After seeing the giant ginger wolf bound down the street, she'd simply gone back inside and yelled at the cat for "attracting the wrong type of customer."

"Well, next time, I'm getting my dumplings to go." Red sniffed but grinned when the infirmary door opened and Cisco stepped back in, bearing a pile of clothes and a belt. He also held up Red's phone, which was chipped but otherwise intact.

"No! What happened to my phone?" Red cried, taking it off Cisco. He switched it on, the dim glow making him sag with relief.

"You dropped it when you turned." Cisco shrugged. "I

tossed the clothes since they were torn to shreds. I got your wallet and your phone, and I saved the four receipts, three old movie tickets, and a giant ball of lint you had hiding in your pocket."

Red grinned. "My lucky lint!"

"Seriously?" Amelia looked at him flatly.

Red held his expression for a minute, then crumbled into laughter. "No. Don't be disgusting. Who'd keep lint on purpose?"

Amelia turned for the door with an exasperated sigh. "Are you allowed to eat? Because you might have had some shut-eye, but we haven't. I love you, but I need coffee."

"I can go get it," Penny said, jumping up. "Cisco, come with. You can help carry them back."

"Can you get me a really, really big coffee?" Red clamored. "And some food. Gods, am I starving!"

Rolling her eyes, Penny gave him a thumbs up and headed for the dining hall, Cisco on her heels.

Once they were out of earshot, Penny slowed. "Cisco, is he gonna be ok?"

"Red's tough," he said. "He'll get through this."

"But, werewolfism?" Penny blew out an irritated breath. "There's no easy cure."

"We just need some wolf's bane." Cisco cocked his head to one side. "Where does that grow, anyway?"

"Cisco, it's poisonous!" Penny walked quickly, letting Cisco jog to catch up. "It's a cure, sure, but it could also kill him."

"Really?" Cisco shook his head. "Damn. I'm sure there's something, though. Werewolves have been around in mythology since, well, forever. Surely *someone* thought there was a cure?"

They'd studied were transformations briefly the previous semester, in Craster's class.

What little Penny knew didn't sound promising. "Were-wolves are an old myth, Cisco. You're right in that. However, unlike Vampires, they didn't come with a whole lot of options for reversing the curse. Many of the old myths were clear that the only way to reverse the curse..."

Was in death.

Cisco got Penny's meaning. "Yeah, well, letting Red die is *not* an option."

"We just have to hope that whatever came through and bit him was a modern interpretation," Penny said. "Movie Weres usually have a failsafe. Or they're gentle, ripped hunks instead of evil child-killers. I wonder if Crenel has anything else?" She pulled out her phone and called him.

The phone rang out. Penny canceled the call before it hit voicemail. "Dammit!"

"Penny, think about it." Cisco opened the dining hall door and stepped back to let her pass through. "Of all the people in the Academy, who do you think March called first? Who would jump at the chance to get his hands on a werewolf, but also want to take care of a student?"

"You mean he's probably already on his way." Penny sighed and nodded. If Crenel wasn't answering, it was because he was already en route. She grabbed a tray and ducked her head to call out the Cook. "We need to take these back to the sickbay. Is that okay?"

"Of course!" Cook hurried over. "Just wait a quick

minute, and I'll have a fresh batch of waffles all ready to go."

Penny leaned against the wall while she waited. It was still early, and the dining hall was almost empty. Yet somehow, Cook had already put out trays of bacon, sausages, and buttered mushrooms. A fresh pot of coffee sat on the counter, steaming gently.

Cisco poured himself a cup while they waited. "Want one?"

Penny nodded and took the fresh cup from him a minute later. "Ugh, I need this."

"Me too." Cisco blew across his cup, then took a sip, closing his eyes with relief.

"Waffles! Here, take a tray and plenty of napkins. Here's a mug of syrup, and don't spill that in the infirmary, mind. Dean March will have my guts for garters!" Cook stacked a tray with platefuls of waffles, syrup, ice cream, and bacon.

Penny eyed it warily. "Bacon...and waffles?"

"No different from pancakes and bacon." Cisco ignored Penny's grimace. He filled two more coffee cups, popped plastic lids on them, and loaded them on the tray. He grabbed it and nodded to Penny. "You'll have to get the door."

Stifling a yawn, Penny led the way back upstairs. Agent Crenel was standing in the doorway and quickly moved to make room for Cisco and Penny. "Sorry I didn't answer," he murmured as Penny passed. "But I figured I'd see you soon enough."

"Room service," Cisco called.

Red was already up. At the sight of food, he grinned.

"You look... better." Penny hadn't realized how much of

Red's easy, relaxed nature had vanished in the last couple of weeks, not until it had returned. His eyes rested on Amelia rather than darting around nervously, and his posture was calm, not ready to pounce.

"I feel better." Red inhaled deeply. "Or at least I will when I get that in me. Is that bacon? I could eat six pigs, trotters and all."

"You're gonna get fat," Amelia warned. "Do you have any idea how much you've been eating since all this happened?"

"That's likely a side effect of the transformation." The woman who spoke paused at the door on her way in. "Good morning, Stuart. I take it this is our patient?"

"Red, I'd like you to meet Doctor Green. She is one of the top biomedical experts in the mythological field." Crenel leaned forward and shook the woman's hand. "It's good to see you, Sarah."

"Not as good as it is to see him." Sarah Green looked at Red with appraising eyes. "You look… Well, perfectly normal, to be honest. You say this all came about because of a scratch?"

"Yup." Red nodded, though his eyes were locked on the tray of food. "When I was lifting the furry bastard, I got me hand caught on one of its big, dribbly fangs."

"What?" Amelia's fists clenched by her sides. "You scratched yourself on a tooth, and you didn't think that was at all relevant?"

Green placed a gentle hand on Amelia's arm. "It's too late to change that," she said. "Red, how do you feel now?"

"Hungry." Red eyes hadn't left the laden tray. Penny wondered if his white-knuckled grip on the mattress was nerves or an attempt to stop himself from attacking Cisco for the tray. "Come on, man. Are you just going to tease me with it?"

"Oh, sorry." Cisco set the tray down on a nearby table and passed Red a plate. Before he had gone back for some cutlery, his friend had half a waffle in his mouth, and three strips of bacon in one hand.

"That's good!" Red exclaimed, his mouth crammed with food.

"Red!" Amelia elbowed him, looking embarrassed on his behalf.

"Let him eat," Doctor Green said kindly. "Stuart is probably right. It's likely that the infection has altered his metabolism. The transformation likely needs a vast amount of energy so he's probably replenishing his depleted stores. Was his appetite unusually high prior to last night?"

Cisco snorted a laugh. "You could say that."

"It certainly doesn't seem to be having a negative effect." Doctor Green ran her eyes over Red's naked torso. He had put his jeans on, but not a shirt.

"Eyes off my boyfriend, lady." Amelia gave the doctor a challenging glare.

"My interest is solely academic, I promise. As much as I'd like to take him home—for *science*—I don't think my wife would approve." Doctor Green grinned at Amelia, who blushed a bright shade of red.

"Sorry," Amelia mumbled.

Doctor Green patted her shoulder. "You were worried about him. It's perfectly understandable."

She perched on the bed next to Amelia. "Let's start from

the very beginning. What happened the night Red was infected?"

Although Penny and her friends hadn't said a word, by the time Red returned to classes the next day, the students were buzzing with gossip about his condition.

"Hey, Red," Myra called as Penny followed him into Madera's class. "Need a scratch behind the ears, boy?"

Clive followed her comment with a mumbled remark about doing it doggy style.

Penny cringed, ready to grab Red if he reacted.

Instead, Red chuckled and let out a howl.

"Not in my class, thank you." Professor Madera strode in, gesturing for the students to sit.

Penny scrambled for a seat.

"Welcome back, Mr. O'Reilly. I hope you're feeling well after your ordeal the other night." The professor glared at the rest of the students. "I hope you will all realize that this is a very real affliction and treat it with the compassion it deserves."

"Come on, professor. I'm not dying. They'll find a cure," Red said happily.

Penny wished she had his confidence. Or his ego. None of the teasing he had endured had taken it down by even a notch. She didn't think she'd be able to endure it half so well.

"Regardless, we have much to discuss today." Madera flicked on a projector, and the image of a website appeared on the whiteboard. The photo of a leprechaun sat next to the headline.

High Court Announces Landmark Case

Paddy O'Paddy, a mythological being residing in Portland, launches his application for legal personhood.

A grin broke over Professor Madera's face. "Students, we are indeed entering a new age. If the applicant succeeds, it may overhaul the current definitions of a 'natural person.' That, in turn, may open the door for the entities crossing the veil to become legally recognized, to apply for citizenship, hold jobs and have equal rights as humans in our country."

"Woohoo!" Red let out a whoop and half the class followed, bursting into excited cheers. Penny's grin widened when she saw everyone in the room at least seemed happy at the revelation.

Everyone except Clive. He raised his hand, a pensive look on his face. "Miss? This is good news and all, but if things keep changing this fast, I've got no chance of passing my exams. I can barely keep the legal stuff straight as it is!"

Madera patted his shoulder. "The current state of affairs will certainly be taken into account at exam time, Clive. I'm not about to dock points for a student not being aware of some obscure law passed the night before the test is given."

Clive looked relieved. "Thanks, Professor."

Madera spent the lesson running over the apparent obstacles the case would face, the arguments the opposition would make, and the ramifications of the possible outcomes.

None of it dampened Penny's joy, not the dry law textbook readings, the tedious research on prior personhood cases, not even the suggestion that Madera might set a lengthy assignment on the topic.

Sensing Penny's excitement, Boots slithered up to her lap and forced her way up between Penny's belly and the edge of the desk. The serpent lifted her head until it was level with Penny's nose.

"Settle down," Penny whispered. "Or you'll get kicked out. But, Boots, do you know what this means?"

Boots swayed her head left to right.

"It means you'll be recognized by the government!" Penny kept her voice low, but Madera had her head down as she rifled through the heavy legal tome on her desk. "It means you'll have rights and protections. You'll be safe from people like those nuts that were protesting last year."

She ignored a twinge of guilt at those words. Boots wouldn't truly be safe. Laws could be broken, and for now, it seemed America and Sweden were the only countries passing them. But it was a damn sight more than she had now. If America led the way, Australia would likely follow, and legal protection would dissuade at least some of the dissenters out there.

Boots licked Penny's chin, but when Madera turned around to address the class, Penny shoved her head back under the table.

"It's all right, Penny." Madera nodded to the stubborn Boots, whose head had popped up again. "I expect she'll be interested in the news, too. Just don't disturb my class, please, dear?" The last words were addressed to the serpent, who gave the professor a happy, bouncing nod. "Thank you. Now, who can give me an example of how corporate personhood might affect the current proceedings?"

Kathy raised her hand but Penny missed her answer, distracted by a cough and a flutter of paper touching the back of her neck. She reached back and grabbed the note from Amelia.

Wanna hit Paddy's on Friday night to celebrate?

Penny put her fist on her shoulder and flicked Amelia a quick thumbs up. Then, she scrawled a word on the scrap of paper before passing it back. *Gift?*

The returning note simply said, *Great idea!* Penny tucked it in her pocket and tried to pull her mind back to the lecture, which had moved on to the expected sequence of events as the case unfolded.

"Listen up, Boots. This could be the best thing that ever happened to the Myther community."

Penny had expected Paddy to be in a celebratory mood. She didn't expect that the whole bar would be decorated to acknowledge the court case, or that it would be busting at the seams with Mythers.

"Aye! It's ma wee human friends! Aye Boots, I didn't forget ye. Come in, come in, ye two-legged bastards!" Paddy ushered them through the door, which was strung with a curtain of shimmering, plastic strips. Inside, a cheap disco ball threw rainbows of light on the walls, giving Penny an immediate headache.

Paddy waved at a nearby faun. "Alf! Get ye cloven trotters over to the bar and grab a few pints for these young 'uns, will ye?"

Alf disappeared, lost in a cluster of toga-clad men and women, two green-faced, hook-nosed witches, and a large black creature with sad eyes and crooked fingers.

"Who's that?" Penny jutted her chin at the monster, unwilling to draw its attention.

"It's the monster under yer bed," Paddy said in a low voice. "Poor bugger. Says he just wants to be friends, but everyone screams and runs away."

"That's so sad." Amelia walked over to the big monster. "Hey, big guy. Can I buy you a drink?"

"Dude, your girlfriend is crazy," Cisco whispered to Red.

"Aye. She is dating a werewolf, though." Red flinched when Paddy jumped up and slapped his back.

"Ah! I knew I could smell somethin' fae on ye! My wee countryman, one of us." Paddy dabbed invisible tears from his eyes with an oversized handkerchief that appeared out of nowhere.

"Uhh, thanks, I guess?" Red shifted awkwardly on the spot, and Paddy slapped a palm against his forehead.

"Ye need a table! Strike me down, Paddy's too distracted to even think. Come, lads—and lass—and I'll find ye a place to sit." He led the way to a corner table. Boots easily dodged the crowd as she followed.

Penny shuffled past the cluster of Greeks, mumbling apologies as she stepped on a sandal-clad toe. When she looked up, she groaned. "You again?"

Bacchus swept his hand wide, and his companions stepped back to let her pass. "You make that sound like a horrible thing."

"Sorry." Penny gave a conciliatory grin. "I just wasn't expecting to see you."

She had to admit that Bacchus himself hadn't really done anything to unsettle her. It was more that his frequent appearances...well, it felt like it meant something. *I'm just pissy because I feel like I'm being left out,* she admitted. With that realization, she felt like a dick.

"Join us," she insisted. *If nothing else, he might know something about cures for werewolfism.*

Bacchus tipped his head up. "Are you sure?"

Penny nodded. "We came to celebrate Paddy. What better way than with the god of celebration?"

"While not entirely correct, I will let that slide." Bacchus waved his hand at the bar staff.

Penny followed him to the table where Red and Cisco were already seated. Paddy stood on a chair, regaling them with the tale of his courtroom drama.

"And I, I said, am presented forthwith to be handin' this here parchment to ye, for the purposes of me provin' meself worthy of bein' a bein'. And the lass, she looked at me with a deadness in her eyes, and she did say that I be in the wrong place, ye see, and that she was only to be seein' to those what had to be payin' a fine for drivin' like a drunken goat."

Bacchus coughed. "My friend, can I offer you a drink in recognition of your victory?" Bacchus pulled a flask seemingly from nowhere, and Paddy accepted it cheerfully.

"Victory?" Penny murmured. "He hasn't won yet."

"No, the victory was finding the damned courthouse to begin with," Bacchus whispered back, mischief in his voice.

"He tried to lodge his application first at the DMV, then at a commercial healing practice."

"I've...never heard a medical surgery described quite like that." Penny covered her grin with her hand before taking a quick gulp of Bacchus's whiskey. It was, like all of the god's liquid creations, exquisite. "You're spoiling me, Bacchus. I won't be able to go back to bottom-shelf spirits after this."

"All the better. I much prefer associating with those of impeccable taste," the god said with a grin. He raised his glass in a toast. "To Paddy!"

The friends cheered the leprechaun, Boots hissing in appreciation with them. Penny downed another drink when her cup refilled itself, raising it to clink against Cisco's glass first.

"Bacchus, what do you know about werewolves?" Penny watched her companion's face carefully as she asked while one hand fumbled in her pocket. She wasn't about to lose a cure for Red's affliction to one of the god's tricks. She readied her phone to record what he might say.

To her dismay, Bacchus shrugged. "Not a great deal, I'm afraid. Tricky beasts. I believe it's one of the few conditions without a viable cure." He chucked Penny under the chin. "But don't fret. It's not such a bad life. Your friend might even come to enjoy it."

Penny chewed her lip. "You said, 'you believe...' Do you mean there *might* be something out there?"

"There could be," Bacchus conceded. "After all, you're drinking with a god. Anything is possible if you believe in it hard enough."

Ignoring the flutter of worry in her gut, Penny changed the subject. "Is everyone here a Myther?"

Bacchus ran his eyes over the room. "Not all. The staff is human, of course. But those two women at the bar? They are witches."

"I got that," Penny said dryly. The pair looked like they had stepped off the set of *The Wizard of Oz*. "Do people really believe that's what witches look like?"

"There was a period of time when that was the case." Bacchus gestured to Amelia, who was still chatting with her new friend. The monster wore a gaping, jagged-edged grin that sent a shiver down Penny's spine. "That one is a combination of childhood myth mixed with a desire to see the good in people. Is it not surprising how many humans not only have faith in a terrible monster out to bite their feet off, but believe him to simply be maligned and misunderstood?"

"I guess it shows how lonely some people are," Penny said quietly. "I can relate to that." Her eyes darted to Cisco, and heat touched her cheeks. "I'm glad I don't feel that way anymore."

"That is Hera and Loki. The older ones, not the child-gods worshipped by the new believers." He gave a circumspect nod to two toga-clad figures whispering in the corner. As if sensing Bacchus' attention, the woman turned cold eyes on him, then stepped delicately to the side so her back faced him as she continued her conversation.

"Over there, the guardian races." Bacchus's eyes slid to a plump, older woman in a wool coat and two tall blonde women with gossamer wings and halos.

"They're what?" Penny wondered what the two angels had to do with the matron-like woman.

"A fairy godmother and two guardian angels." As he spoke, the matron wriggled her coat off to reveal tiny sparkling wings on her back. She nodded in agreement with one of the angels, then plucked a wand from her pocket and gave it a twitch. A steaming mug appeared on the table and she took a sip, her rosy cheeks brightening with glee.

The bell over the door tinkled, and it swung open. A dog—at least, it looked a little like a dog—leaped through and up onto a table, turning its long, sculpted nose toward Bacchus. Even seated, its tail stood stiffly upright to show off a forked tip.

"Ah, Sha is here. I must go speak to him." Bacchus slid his chair back and gave Penny an apologetic bow. "Please excuse me." He left and joined the canine-like creature at another table.

"Ah, he left before fillin' me cup!" Paddy cursed, then hooted with delight when his glass began to fill from an invisible source. "My favorite god, that one. Well, apart from me own."

"Who are your gods, Paddy?" Penny asked. "Is it the Tuatha de Danann?" Her tongue tripped over the Gaelic, unable to pronounce the name as Red had tried to teach her.

"Aye, but don't let them hear ye butcher their name like that, lass!" Paddy stepped over a bowl of fries on the table to come nearer. "Their wrath be mighty and swift."

"Oh." Penny glanced around nervously, wondering if the vengeful fae were present.

"Don't ye worry." Paddy stepped back with a grin and jabbed a thumb over his shoulder. "They're out back."

"What is this place," Cisco asked. "A Myther refugee center?"

Paddy opened his mouth, paused, then nodded. "Aye. More or less."

"Paddy, who knows about this?" Penny asked, alarmed. "Humans, I mean?"

Paddy gave her a quizzical glance. "Why wouldn't we tell the humans?"

"Because having a giant influx of Mythers in a bar could attract, I don't know, trouble?" Penny's stomach filled with dread at the idea of protesters turning up to cause trouble. "Especially now your face is all over the news."

"Ah." Paddy dropped his eyes, scuffing the toes of his boot on the table. "I hadn't thought of that."

"Look, we can put you in touch with someone who can keep this haven a safe place for Mythers," Penny said. She caught Cisco's eye. "Can't we?"

Cisco quickly agreed. "I'm sure Dean March will know who to tell."

"Well, I'll have to check with me compatriots." Paddy hopped down into the seat Bacchus had vacated. "But that does seem like a mighty fine idea."

"Hey, guys. Got room for two more?" Amelia leaned down to nudge Red over and pulled up a chair for herself, while the looming void of darkness beside her stood there awkwardly.

"Uhh, sure." Penny scooted over and leaned back to snatch another chair from a vacant table. "Here you go."

She had to squish further over to make room for the

creature when he sat, his bigness puddling around him as he folded himself into the chair.

"Want a drink, buddy?" Cisco asked. Shot a glance at Amelia, eyebrows raised.

"Paddy'll get ye something, Munder. Milk?"

The monster nodded slowly. Beside him, Boots hissed.

"Fine, two pots of milk it is. Not one of ye have an ounce of taste, ye know."

"Munder?" Penny asked.

"Aye. Monster Under the bed. Get it?" The leprechaun cackled at his own ingenuity. "Munder!"

Munder trembled with what Penny hoped was a chuckle. "Do not forget the milk, little green one. And a cookie, if it is not too much trouble."

His voice was gravelly and sent prickles over Penny's skin, but she tried to ignore it for the sake of their guest.

"Aye, milk and a cookie, ye big scary bastard." Paddy shook his head disparagingly. "Why anyone would be scared of yer soggy arse I don't know. Milk and bloody cookies!"

He stomped off, and Munder trembled again. "Little green one gives me the belly laughs. Funny little one."

"And to think, for all those years, I was too scared to dangle my foot off the bed," Penny murmured. "If only I'd known you were friendly."

Munder turned slowly toward her. "I was not under your bed, Serpent-friend. The monster in your dreams would eat your toes and feast on your eyeballs if you met him today."

"Oh." Penny swallowed hard.

"He is very polite, though." Munder's gaping mouth

widened, although Penny couldn't be sure if it was a smile or gas. "And he does like a game of chess with Munder on the rare occasions we do meet."

The beast trembled again, then turned to strike up a conversation with Amelia.

"I'm never sleeping again," Penny whispered to Cisco. "Seriously. Can you come check under my bed when we get home?"

"Only if you let me bring a flamethrower." Even Cisco had lost color, although Amelia still seemed happy, and Red... "Hey." Cisco looked around. "Where'd Red go?"

"For that matter, where's Boots?" Penny joined him, craning her neck to try to see through the crowded bar.

Paddy was on his way back with a tray of whiskey, milk, and cookies, but the serpent was nowhere to be found.

"Over there." Cisco pointed. Red was at a nearby table talking to a slender, fair-skinned woman in a white dress. "Who the hell is that?"

"Is that *Boots*?" Penny squinted at the lump on the table. When it twitched and raised a head, she tsked. "It *is* Boots. Who the hell are they talking to?"

"Who?" Paddy slid the tray onto the table and looked over his shoulder. "Vila? Ah, don't be worryin' about her. She's one of us."

Still watching her friends, Penny took a sip of whiskey. It bit harder than Bacchus's brew, and her head was already a little muzzy. So, when she watched the young woman stand up and shed her dress, her first instinct was to giggle.

"Cisco. You wouldn't *believe* the hallucination I'm having right now."

Cisco didn't laugh. Rather, he blushed bright red, his

eyes bulging as he watched the naked Vila gesture to Red. "Try me."

"Penny. Hold my drink." Amelia, mouth set in a furious line, shoved her chair back and slammed her drink on the table.

"Wait. She's really naked, isn't she?" Penny glanced back just in time to see Vila's transformation.

Vila raised her arms and pressed her palms together. Her hands lengthened and her body contorted in a graceful twist, wrapping around on itself and coiling into a pile next to Boots. When Boots nudged it, a snake's head popped up, this one black and glittering.

The new snake unwound, slithered to the floor, and changed again in a writhing movement. Its body swelled and sprouted legs and a tail. A shimmering wave passed over it as gray fur rippled. The snake, now a bristling wolf, cocked its head at Red and lifted a paw.

Amelia sat back down with a thump. "Paddy? What the fuck was that?"

"She'd be showin' loverboy how to shift without makin' a mess," Paddy said. "What, ye didn't expect her to be tearin' up her dress, did ye?"

"I...guess not." Brow still wrinkled with a frown, Amelia picked her drink back up and gulped the rest down. "But if she sniffs his butt again, she gets the hose."

Paddy clapped his hands. "Oh, that'd be a sight to see! Two fine lasses from opposing side of the Veil, facin' off in a battle to the death!"

Amelia flinched. "I didn't say I'd *kill* her."

"Aye, but if ye piss her off, she wouldn't be so generous." Paddy chuckled. "Not to worry, lass. I'm sure ye could take her. Maybe not enough to lay a coin in yer favor, but enough to cheer ye on enthusiastically at least."

Amelia narrowed her eyes at the leprechaun. "Paddy, I'd highly advise you stop talking before *you* get the hose."

Paddy chuckled, the sound fading as he realized Amelia might be serious. "Ah. Oh, well, ahh..." He cast his eyes around, desperate for something to change the conversation. "What have ye all been doin' with yer time, then? It's been an age since Paddy has seen ye all."

"Studying, mostly," Cisco said. "Red's been enduring test after test as they look for a cure for fleas." He dodged a punch from Amelia.

"I've been job-hunting," Penny chimed in morosely. "You don't know of anything, do you?"

"Ye want a job?" Paddy tipped his head up and let out a screech. "PADDY! WHERE ARE YE, PADDY?"

The bar fell silent. Paddy raised his head to scream again when a shout rang out. "I'm coming, you pain-in-the-ass leprechaun."

The man that approached the table was...well, human, at least in appearance. Penny eyed him warily. "You're Paddy?"

"Joshua, actually." He stuck out a hand and Penny shook it, his grip firm. "I've told him that a thousand times, but the little prick still calls me Paddy."

"Why?" Cisco asked.

Joshua shrugged. "Because I own the bar."

"You told me the bar was yours." Penny slapped the back of Paddy's head, sending his hat tumbling to the ground.

He jumped down and snatched it up haughtily. "It is. In a manner of speaking. At least, it's named after me."

"That's bullshit," Joshua said dryly. "You know we only tolerate you because people drink more when you're here, right?"

"That's what ye say, but deep down, I know ye love me." Paddy fluttered his eyes at the bar owner, who stared back, unimpressed.

"What do you want, Paddy?" Joshua finally asked.

"This here wee lass needs a job. I know ye been lookin' for someone, so I found ye one!" Paddy waved his hands, presenting Penny as if she were a prize on a game show.

"I'm sorry, Joshua," Penny said quickly. "I only mentioned I was looking. I didn't mean for him to—"

"What are your qualifications?" Joshua asked. He took Red's seat and rested his elbows on the table.

"Uh. Not much, to be honest. I've worked a few places, but never in a bar." Put on the spot, Penny's brain scrambled to assemble the facts she'd recited at her half-dozen interviews so far.

Joshua leaned back in his chair, an appraising look in his eyes. "You kids are all from that creepy Academy place, aren't you?"

"I wouldn't call it creepy," Penny protested.

"Except for the dead guy's hand, the psychotic gnome, the serial-killer doll, and the incident with the Sasquatch," Cisco added with a grin.

"You've got the job." Joshua stood.

"What?" Penny almost fell off her seat. "Just like that?"

"Yeah, just like that. You start tomorrow, midday. Paddy's people have some kind of meeting on, and I'll need the extra staff." Without looking back, Joshua headed back to the bar. "Don't be late!"

Penny tried to wipe the giant grin off her face but quickly gave up. She downed her whiskey and waved the empty glass at Paddy. "I don't know whether to thank you or thump you."

"Ye can thank me, lass. Paddy is a fair man to work for. He'll push ye hard, but he'll treat ye well."

"Think about it, hon," Amelia reached over to put a hand on Penny's arm. "He must be a nice guy if he puts up with this little shit." She winked at Paddy and laughed at his outraged glare.

"Ye friend does have a fair point there," Paddy admitted. "But in all honesty, I should be gettin' back to work. Thank ye for the celebratin' and well wishin'."

Penny watched him go, a jumble of nervous excitement in her gut.

CHAPTER THIRTEEN

"Listen, Granny." Penny rested her hands flat on the table and leaned over, her face level with the Fairy Godmother. "I don't care what alliances you're making or who you think deserves to be in it. In *this* bar, you play by *our* rules."

"What are you going to do to me if I don't, child?" For all her kind old woman persona, the old lady sure had a stubborn streak.

Penny picked up the salt shaker and sprinkled a few grains on the table. When Esmerelda's eyes flicked to them, frantically counting the scattered grains, Penny allowed herself a small smile. Her research had paid off.

"I have about twenty pounds of salt out back. How far do you think your little alliance will go if you have to spend the next three years counting grains?"

The godmother paused. Then she sniffed, scowling. "Fine. Uriel, Michael? We shall find somewhere else to conduct business."

"Hey, you're welcome to stay." Penny spread her hands.

"But if I see you hassling Munder one more time, I'll kick your ass. You don't want Little Jimmy to be at the mercy of his bullies, do you?"

The two angels stood. The taller one bowed to Penny. "We apologize for any disturbance. Esmeralda's heart is in the right place, she just—"

"Don't you even try apologizing on my behalf, you impotent bag of feathers." The godmother threw her coat on, reaching back to adjust her wings. "We're leaving. I won't abide a place that welcomes beasts like him."

She snatched her wand off the table and stormed out. Rather than follow, the angels watched her go. "Might I trouble you for a pint?" The shorter one asked.

"I'm not the bartender, but I can ask her for you," Penny explained. Though she had expected her position to involve pouring drinks or washing dishes, Joshua had instead explained that the vacant position was for a bouncer. Although her smaller build would make her a laughable security person at a normal bar, the skills she was learning at the Academy, along with her friendships with Paddy and Bacchus, made her the perfect person for the job.

Before she headed to the bar, Penny gathered up their empty glasses, wondering how much damage she had caused to whatever alliance the angels had been formulating with the fairy godmother. "Sorry about your friend." She ducked her head and hurried over to the bar.

Since Penny had begun her shift—and while trying to adjust to a job that was not at all what she'd anticipated—the Fairy Godmother had been needling Munder with insults, trying to get him riled enough for Joshua to order him out.

Instead, Munder had retreated further and further into himself until Penny had snapped. *If you're gonna make me a bouncer, then I'll bounce,* Penny had decided.

In fairness, her only instruction had been to keep the peace in whatever way she needed to. Munder's plight had begun to attract attention from a gaggle of gnomes by the pool table, and Penny didn't want to have to deal with a brawl on her first day.

"Everything okay?" Joshua appeared beside her, and Penny gave him a quick rundown of what had happened.

"I hope I didn't overstep." Penny held her breath, waiting for Joshua to tear her a new one for kicking out one of their classier patrons.

"Good job." Joshua grabbed the empty beer mugs off the table and whisked them back to the bar, Penny on his heels. "Honestly, if I'd known that throwing a bag of salt at the old bitch would have shut her up, I'd have done it months ago."

Relieved, Penny leaned over the bar. "The angels want a pint each. Want me to take it over to them?"

Joshua shook his head. "You need your hands free, I'll send one of the girls out. Thanks for letting me know."

Penny wandered back out to let Michael and Uriel know their drinks were on the way.

The older of the two angels offered up a quick prayer on her behalf. "Many thanks, child."

Penny lifted an eyebrow. "Child? I'm twenty-two."

"And I'm four hundred and twenty-eight billion years old." He smiled. "To me, you are but a child. A tiny babe."

"Oh. Well, I guess that's fair." Penny sidled away, unsure if she was more awed or insulted. She headed over to check on Munder. "You okay, mate?"

"I am o-kaaay." He stared morosely at his half-eaten cookie. "It would be so nice if the Fairy Godmother did not hate me so much."

"She's a stuck-up bitch," Penny shot back. "Don't worry about her. How's the cookie?"

"It is nice." He took another nibble, the smoky wisps of his fingers allowing several crumbs to fall through. "Sorry. I am crumbling a mess."

"It's cool." Penny darted over to the bar and returned with a napkin. "Here."

"You are so very helpful." Munder gaped his mouth in what Penny was now sure was a grin.

"No worries!" The doors to the back room opened. "Gotta run." She headed toward the mass of...*well, people, I guess,* she told herself.

Only, these people were mostly leprechauns, ghosts, angels, monsters, gods, and a whole lot more Penny didn't recognize. Among them, Penny spied a couple of familiar faces in the crowd. Special Agents Crenel and Delouise passed before she could grab their attention.

"Penny!" Paddy waved her over. Beside him, Boots reached up to watch the alliance members leaving.

"Hey, Paddy." Penny reached down to scratch Boots' head. "Hey, sweet girl. Anything interesting happen in there?"

"Of a sort, lass." Paddy's face was lit up like a beacon, his happiness practically leaking out of him. "I got meself a guarantee of funding for me court case, and your people said they'll be happy to help me not get meself killed on the way in an' out."

"That's promising," Penny said. "What about the alliance?"

"Well, there's still a whole lot of details to be sortin' out, like who can be a part and who needs a wee kick in the knackers first... but we're gettin' there."

A tall black man squeezed past her, his heavy gilt crown and thick robes taking up more space than the suited man trailing him.

The second man stopped, eyeing Penny. "Friend, might I inquire as to your name?"

"It's Penny." She pursed her lips, wondering what the hell kind of mythological being dressed like a lawyer.

"Ah, Penny." He pulled a clipboard out of nowhere and ran an expensive ballpoint down the list. "Penny, Penny... Here. Penny Smith? Penny Walker? Penny Jones?"

"None of those." She leaned forward, trying to get a peek at the papers. "Why?"

"I have a number of clients who are sadly deceased." The man gave her a sparkling smile. "Unfortunately their fortunes are tied up due to a lack of heirs. If I could just find an American citizen who shares their legal name..." He gave a dramatic sigh. "Of course, such a citizen would be compensated very—"

"Stop." Penny held her hands up. "Just stop. I don't want to know." He tried to talk again, and she snapped a hand up. "Not a *word!* I have never wanted to slap my grandmother more than I do right now," she muttered.

Her nan had, before she died, been an absolute sucker for every scam that made it past her email filters, from "click here to fix your virus" messages to Nigerian royalty looking to marry, and…

Oh, shit.

Penny looked around for the man's companion. She spied him kneeling at a table where an old woman had a hand pressed to her chest.

"Oh, no." She bolted over just in time to catch the words "fortune will be yours" leave the man's lips.

"Out!" She yanked him up by the scruff of his opulent collar. "Out, and take your scummy lawyer with you. No, I don't care if you're the real deal. You're *not* finding a bride in this bar."

The prince tried to hold a ring box out to her.

Penny pointed at the door. "Oh, *hell,* no! OUT!"

Chagrined, the two men left without harassing any more customers. Penny turned to the old lady watching them leave.

"I could have been a princess," she whispered, chin trembling.

"I'll comp you a drink," Penny said hurriedly. "What'll it be?"

"Oh. Uh, I'll take a gin and tonic, please." Still watching the now-empty doorway, the woman gave a tremulous smile. "Well, I suppose my husband wouldn't have approved anyway."

She twisted the wedding ring on her finger. "Just imagine, me going home to tell him I need a divorce so I can marry a wealthy foreign prince!"

"Good grief." Penny headed over to the bar to explain the situation to Janice, the waitress.

"Not the first time that's happened here." Janice sighed

as she poured the woman's drink. "Last one was left heart-broken when he proposed to three other women before he left. Three! Can you believe that?"

"Yes. I can." Penny stepped away from the bar as the door opened and two small fairies flew through.

Let's hope they're not assholes like the godmother. In all honesty, though, the prospect didn't bother her. She knew Josh had her back, and she had to admit, acting as peace-keeper in a bar full of Mythers was more suited to Penny's temperament than pulling drinks or making coffee would have been.

Most importantly, the schedule was flexible. *The pay is good, too,* Penny mused. Josh had given her a contract to sign before her shift, offering Penny quite a bit more than she'd have earned as a waitress. *I just hope it works out.*

———

The next week passed quickly. Glass had spent a class teaching the students how to grapple. Fitness was spent climbing ropes in the first lesson and doing laps at a local pool the next.

"How are you going to hunt water-based Mythers if you struggle to tread water?" Glass yelled at Mara.

Mara actually wasn't a bad swimmer, as long as her head was above water. Each time she tried to go under, she would immediately surface, spluttering and coughing.

"I just can't, okay?" She climbed out of the pool to face off with the professor. "It gets up my nose, and I panic. I don't like it any more than you do!" She snatched her towel up and made to storm off, shaking off Glass as he tried to grab her arm on her way past. "Asshole."

"Mara, you step out of this facility, and you fail this class." Glass barked the command loud enough for even Penny to jump.

Mara turned back and raised a finger, mouth opened to argue.

"I didn't say you have to get back in the pool." He walked over to her, hands on his hips. "Now, you're not gonna get past this by ignoring it. The way I see it is, you've got two options here. You can work past your fear, or you can sit out this task and hope like hell you ace the rest of the course, then continue hoping like hell that you never get attacked by an amphibious Myther or a sentient showerhead."

Mara scowled, folding her arms over her chest. She did not, however, argue.

Glass lowered his voice, turning his back on the classmates as he continued chatting to Mara. "Now, I'm prepared to give up my own time to help you with this if you choose the option that won't get you killed. Six AM, Monday, Wednesday, and Friday. Right here."

A moment later, after a sniffling Mara had nodded in agreement to his proposal, Glass swung back around. "What the hell are you doing? Laps, people, laps! You're not a group of dead goldfish, so get swimming!"

Penny threw herself off the wall and kicked her legs, propelling her underwater. *Glass might be an asshole, but he's actually kinda nice when it counts.* She broke the surface of the water again, breaking into a breaststroke to reach the other end.

"I could throw a bucket of lard into this pool and it would float better than you." Glass spat the words at Trevor, who was flailing in one corner of the pool, trying to do as instructed. "No! Not like that, you underfed bean pod. Put your legs... Oh, my God, I'm working with imbeciles."

Penny dove back under before Glass could yell at her again for eavesdropping. *Yup. Definitely an asshole.*

Three hours later, Penny was dry, dressed, and crammed into the back of a van with Clive, Cisco, and Jason.

The van lurched around a corner, and Penny had to grip the tiny desk next to her for balance. Cisco, however, had nothing to grab.

He sprawled across her lap, his hands gripping her knees to right himself.

"Careful what you're grabbing there, mate." Penny could see he was doing his best not to screw up, but she couldn't resist the jab. "I know Clive is having a good old fondle over there, but that doesn't mean I'm ready for the next step in our relationship yet."

"No, I'm not!" Across from her, Clive snatched his hands away from Jason before he could be accused of any more wrongdoing.

"Goddammit Clive, get off!" Jason shoved his partner, almost sending him tumbling into the cupboards full of expensive surveillance gear.

The van screeched to a halt. A minute later, Quaid yanked open the back door.

"Oh, for God's sake. Stop groping each other and get out." He stepped back and waited for the students to pile out of the van.

"Grab my balls like that again, and I'll kick your head so hard your teeth will fall out of your ass," Jason muttered.

"Chill, Jason." Penny breezed by him, stepping out into the afternoon sunlight. "That was your own hand on your dick."

"No, it—"

"Mate, I was sitting straight across from you. He bumped your elbow, that's all." She grinned when Jason flushed and grumbled a weak apology to his class partner.

"Today, you're working in a four-man team." Quaid narrowed his eyes at Penny as if daring her to point out— for the third time that day—that she was a woman.

She smiled sweetly back.

Quaid gave an almost disappointed huff. "Like I was saying. You work together, and you get the target out. I'm not stepping in to help you this time. In fact, I'm on the other team, so watch your asses."

He explained the task. "You use the equipment in the van to activate a device on the top floor of the abandoned apartment block across the road. The building is rigged with alarms and cameras, and I'm going to be running interference."

The groan from the students made Quaid smile. "Timer starts in five. You can check your gear while it runs. You got thirty after that to succeed. Go!"

Penny hit the timer on her phone before Quaid vanished to do whatever it was that Quaid did when he ran interference on one of their tasks. "Timer set!"

She dove for the desk, yanking out the drawers to grab radios for each of them.

Cisco already had the cupboard open. "Sweet! We got a bot!"

Penny punched the air. "Yes! That'll make this a breeze."

"Seriously?" Jason took a radio. "If he gave us a bot, he's got a dozen anti-bot devices. I swear to god the guy is only here to set us up to fail."

"We don't always fail," Penny pointed out. "We won the last challenge."

"Yeah, our first win out of ten." Clive inserted an earpiece and tucked the wire down his shirt. "What else have we got?"

The team quickly discussed their equipment, Penny's timer pinging to let them know they could exit the van.

"I have a plan." Penny grinned. "It'll require all of us on board."

Jason tipped his head up. "Are you using the bot?"

She grinned. "Of course. If he really did bring all that gear, I wouldn't wanna disappoint him."

CHAPTER FOURTEEN

Ten minutes later, the tiny screen in the van went blank. "He's got the bot!" She hissed into her mic.

At the twenty-minute mark, Quaid had Penny face down on the floor, hands cuffed behind her back.

"Did you just give up?" Quaid asked as he helped her to her feet. "Because that was a stupid move. You walked right in here without even checking for booby traps!"

"I never give up." She flashed her instructor a grin.

"Then what—" Quaid flinched as music blared nearby, a screeching techno beat that made Penny wish she'd thought to grab earplugs. "Oh."

Quaid gave Penny an appreciative nod, then bolted from the room. She couldn't follow since he'd pronounced her officially dead when she'd stumbled on the room he had been hiding in, tripped an alarm, then snagged herself in a false trap that would have garrotted her if it was for real.

"Please, work, please work." A minute later, there was a

hoot of delight. "Yes!" Penny sprang up from the ground, certain they had won the challenge.

"Aww, dammit!" Jason's curse rang through the abandoned halls.

"Shit." Jason had been tasked to get the package. *He shouldn't even be on this floor!* Penny realized with frustration.

The plan was for Jason to shinny up the fire escape while Quaid was distracted with the other team members' false attempts to secure it from the inside.

Suddenly, music blared through a nearby speaker—*We Are The Champions*. Penny nursed the glimmer of hope that had flared at the sound. Quaid was known for his love of Queen, and his unusual ways of letting the students know if they had passed or failed a task.

A holler of victory soon confirmed it, and Quaid returned to the small room to uncuff Penny's wrists.

"Technically a win," Quaid said. "But you lost three-quarters of your damn team. Try that in the field, and no one will work with you—ever."

"You always tell us to weigh the 'real world' consequences, Professor." Penny rubbed her wrists. "In the real world, the consequence is getting tagged in a game of stuck in the mud, not a funeral."

"Smartass kids." Quaid shoved the cuffs back into his pocket and stomped away.

"I don't think he likes losing." Cisco stuck his head in the doorway. "You coming? We're gonna get pizza."

"I can't." Penny smothered a yawn just thinking about it. "I had to work late last night. There was a poltergeist pissing about in the bar, and he would *not* leave. It took me two bags of salt, four prayers, and a cricket bat to get the bastard out."

Cisco did his best impression of puppy-dog eyes. "Come on. We won't be out late."

"Fine. But I'm heading home at eight. I don't care if we're not done." Penny pushed away the feeling that she'd regret it in the morning. "You'd better bring me coffee before class tomorrow."

"It's a deal." Cisco thrust his hand out for her to shake. "I'll even buy you a drink at the pizza joint."

———

When Cisco turned up at Penny's room at seven the following morning with a croissant and a coffee, she was glad she had pre-organized it.

Her head throbbed from too many cheap drinks the night before, and she had a vague recollection of tumbling through the door close to midnight, much later than the eight PM deadline she had promised.

When she arrived at advanced driver skills class, Clive looked on her with pity.

"Rough night?" he asked, nodding at the empty coffee cup in her hand.

To Penny's disgust, Jason and Clive seemed fine. Cisco at least had the grace to look a little worn around the edges. His hair stuck out at odd angles, and his brown skin had a hint of sallow green to it.

"You mind if I show you something quickly?" Clive asked. He gestured for Penny to follow him.

Clive grabbed the rucksack he took everywhere he went, pulling the top flap aside to reveal a brass goblet.

"What's that?" Penny asked, suddenly wary.

"A gift from an...*associate* of the Academy." Clive winked.

"Bacchus." Penny said the god's name with a hint of dryness.

Nodding, Clive passed her the cup and murmured, "I got too drunk, and it's time for class. Oh, mighty Bacchus, save my ass."

The goblet bubbled as it filled with clear liquid, then stilled. Penny sniffed it timidly. "How exactly did you get this?"

"At a party a few weeks ago. Bacchus was there, and we got to talking. He seems personally offended at the concept of being hungover." Clive shrugged, almost spilling the magical drink. "So he gave me this and told me the prayer that would activate it."

"He told you to pray with the word 'ass?'" Penny asked.

Clive seemed to miss her skeptical tone. "Real joker, that guy. Here, drink up before Mack comes looking for us."

Penny took the cup hesitantly. *What the hell, I can't feel any worse than I do.* She downed it in a few gulps and handed the cup back to Clive, her head already clearer now that the throbbing ache had vanished.

"Wow." She blinked, the world seeming less bright and angry. "That really works."

"Are you two coming, or what?" Mack yelled. "Get on the bus."

The trip to the driving track was short, and before long, Penny sat astride a motorbike, glaring at the track ahead.

She knew this track like the back of her hand and had the best safety equipment money could buy. That didn't stop the nerves worming in her gut. This was their third lesson on two wheels, and she still didn't have the hang of it.

"Remember, only go as fast as you feel comfortable, but speed is balance." Mack waved a red flag. "Go!"

Penny twisted the accelerator, and the bike took off. She crested the first hill, slowing so that the wheels stayed in contact with the dirt track.

Picking up speed on the other side, Penny gritted her teeth as the bike sped up the next hill. She pushed it harder, and she rose off the seat as the ground dropped away.

For a moment, she was flying.

Then she hit the ground hard, and the last thing she experienced before she blacked out was a jolt to the bike's handlebars that shoved the front wheel to one side and sent her sprawling.

When Penny opened her eyes again, all she saw was the cloud of dust drifting past between her and the bright blue sky.

"Shit!" She pulled herself out from under the bike as Mack rushed over, carrying the Asclepius staff. She waved it away.

"Just my pride." Penny tore the helmet off and shook her hair out. "I don't know what it is. I just suck on two wheels."

Mack shook his head. He had a rule about self-disparaging comments in his class, although this time, he let it slide. "You just need to get to know her. Look, it's only twenty minutes until the end of class. Go get yourself a drink and when we're done, you can take her out on your own."

Penny pulled back. "Are you sure that's a good idea? What if I break it?"

"Just don't kill yourself." Mack pointed to a section of the track near the barn. "Head out that way until you get to the gate. Go through it, and follow the path into the forest reserve. There's a great little track through there, not too challenging. It might help you get a feel for the bike, though, and have some fun with it."

Penny nodded, although she was unsure whether Mack's confidence in her was entirely warranted. She headed toward the small camp set up, where a large cooler of electrolyte drink sat beside the mountain of sandwiches that Mack bought every week.

He had been right that a cold drink and something to eat would make her feel a little better. Penny sat and watched the final student do his run on the bike. Cisco was always her favorite to watch.

He took off much as she had, moving slowly over the first hill and picking up speed for the jump beyond it. Unlike Penny, though, Cisco landed his jump perfectly, zooming to take off at the second. His run was over in a few short minutes, much to Penny's disappointment. She could have sat there and watched him ride all day.

She admonished herself. *You're not Amelia. Get a grip, girl.*

The class ended, and Penny's fellow students headed toward her to start packing up. The sandwiches were quickly eaten, since the three hungry young men always made short work of whatever snacks were available. Once the folding table was packed on the bus, Mack nodded to Penny.

"Are you gonna take the bike, or are you wimping out on me?" he asked.

Penny raised an eyebrow. "Me? Wimp out? You don't know me very well, do you?"

"I was hoping I did, and I'm glad I was right." Mack gave Penny a fist-bump. "I have to get these three idiots back to the Academy. When you're done, ride the bike back. I'll have Jess organize someone to return it."

Penny nodded, reflexively trying not to put a hand on her stomach when her nerves fluttered. *It's an easy track,* she reminded herself. *He wouldn't send me out there if I was likely to get injured. Not on my own, anyway.* She knew it was true. Mack might be a little crazy, but he'd never put any of them in danger.

Mack left with the three boys leaning out of the bus window to holler good luck wishes at Penny. When they were gone, she turned to the little red bike.

"We can do this the easy way or the hard way," she told it. 'If we're out on some little goat track together and I fall off, *you're* going to get left to rust in the rain. Yes, I know it's not raining. But I'll make sure you were buried so deep in the forest no one will ever find you got it?"

The bike sat silently.

"Glad we understand each other." Penny swung her leg over and flicked the kickstand up with her heel. "Let's go."

She rode slowly past the track used for training, past the old barn where she had jumped a car and taken out a cardboard zombie, and over to the little gate. As Mack had promised, it was unlocked. She pushed it open and wheeled the bike through.

The track was indeed an easy meandering path through the forest. The gentle curves and easy rises and dips gave Penny the confidence to increase her speed.

Pine needles and spindly branches whipped past at an increasing pace. Twice, she scared birds that had been minding their own business, sitting on branches that crossed over the trail.

This isn't so bad, Penny realized. She was deep in the forest now, glad that her path had only been a single track. Otherwise, she wasn't sure she'd have been able to find her way back.

Penny slowed when she reached a tiny clearing. She killed the engine and took her helmet off, then inhaled the pine-scented air deeply. "I could almost get to enjoy this."

A twig snapped next to her. Penny froze.

She heard the snorting exhale of a deep breath and slowly turned her head. Not ten feet away, a majestic white horse stood in the trees. It pawed the ground with one hoof and let out a gentle snort. When it ducked its head to tap a thin, spiraling horn on the hard-packed dirt, Penny gasped.

"You're a unicorn!" Penny's mind fled back to her childhood when, like every other girl she knew, she'd dreamed of owning her very own unicorn.

Penny took a slow step forward, one hand outstretched toward the mythical beast.

The unicorn whinnied and took a step back.

"It's okay, bud," Penny said soothingly. She took another step, but the unicorn dodged away again.

Penny let her hand fall away, stifling her disappointment. *I've seen it,* she told herself. *That's enough.* She edged back toward her bike, and to her surprise, the unicorn pranced joyfully.

"Wait a minute..." Penny cocked her head to one side, watching the eager unicorn. "You want to run with me?"

It danced again, and Penny carefully slid her helmet back over her head. She threw one leg over her bike and turned the engine, wincing when it rumbled to life. It didn't bother her new friend, though.

Penny tested her theory by inching forward slowly at first, gaining speed when the unicorn kept pace with her.

As Penny's bike flew past the trees once more, the unicorn gave a joyful whinny. Its thundering hoof beats kept pace with the roar of the bike as the two of them sped through the forest.

The path began to get tighter and harder to navigate. The trail was less traveled here, and more prone to dipping through gullies and over crooked humps.

Penny wrenched the handlebars and skidded around a tight corner. She glanced back to check on her friend.

The unicorn tossed its head, unbothered by the change in direction.

Penny pulled her attention back to the track. "Oh, *fuck.*" The gully was too close to avoid. Her stomach dropped, just like the solid ground beneath her, then slammed against her diaphragm. The bike shot up the other side and into the air.

Breathing shallowly, Penny was only vaguely aware of the large white shape sailing across the gully beside her.

Hooves landed with a clatter a moment before the bike's wheels hit the dirt in perfect alignment. Penny gently hit the brakes and slid to a stop, heart racing.

"That...was...*amazing!*" She jerked her head up when the unicorn reared, front feet lifted high, tail swishing. It bounded over to the trees and vanished into the foliage, its hoofbeats fading into the distance as it galloped away.

Penny took a moment to catch her breath, sucking in gasps as she tried not to sob. The magical experience had touched her, but more than that, she'd finally moved past whatever had been stopping her from landing her jumps on the bike.

"I did it," she said, her voice soft. "I really did it."

CHAPTER FIFTEEN

R ed tore into another chicken leg with his teeth. "You're sure it wasn't just a horse with a stick in its hair?"

"No, Red." Penny gave him a withering glare. "I know a unicorn when I see one."

"You know," Amelia said, absentmindedly handing Red a napkin to wipe the sauce off his face, "I always wanted a unicorn when I was a kid."

"Who didn't?" Penny grinned, her elation still fluttering in her heart.

"Uh, me?" Red raised his hand. "I wanted a T-rex or a battle robot. Or maybe a big tank that shoots bombs and has its own wee refrigerator inside, so I don't have to go out to get soda."

"Wow. That's…really specific." Amelia took a sip of her drink and burped discreetly.

"Amelia!" Red leaned back in a show of disgust. "Did you have to? Now the poor agent is going to have to arrest you for the public expulsion of toxic gas!"

Amelia shook her head, looking up over Penny's shoulder. "Sorry, Agent Crenel. The werewolf thing has made him go a bit cuckoo. Then again, he *was* born dumb."

Penny swung around in her seat to see Crenel standing behind her, doing his best to look as though he hadn't found the exchange hilarious. He coughed and looked away for a moment, then addressed Penny.

"Miss Hingston, might I have a word?"

"Sure." Penny slid her plate over to Red, who eyed her last bit of fried chicken hungrily. "Go for it, Red. I'm full anyway."

Penny followed the unusually silent agent through the halls of the Academy, all the way back to his tiny office. Once they were inside, Crenel closed the door.

"How are things?" Crenel leaned on his desk, arms folded as he looked down on Penny. "I heard you got a job at Paddy's."

Penny nodded. She hadn't had a chance to catch up with the agent since seeing him at the meeting Paddy had organized. "I started last week. It's good money, and I needed the work."

"Is it safe?" he asked.

Penny cocked her head. "Sure. Most of the Mythers there are pretty friendly. They'd back me up if I needed it, I'm sure. If not for my sake, then for the bar itself. Dean March explained about it being a safe haven?"

Crenel gave a brisk nod. "Paddy is becoming quite the celebrity." He dropped his arms, adopting a more casual pose. "After Jessica spoke to me about the situation, I went to see him. He has big plans for a tiny guy."

"I saw you at the meeting," Penny admitted. "What happened in there?"

"A lot of talk, mostly. Paddy is trying to get the Mythers —the non-homicidal ones, anyway—to agree to an alliance. If they present a united front, agree to adhere to the laws we humans have in place... Well, it'll make things a lot easier on them, legally speaking." Crenel folded his arms again, looking impatient.

"You didn't bring me here to talk about that," Penny guessed.

"No." Crenel sighed, screwing up his mouth like he tasted something bad. "I need to ask you some questions."

"About?" Penny darted a glance at the door, wondering if she was in trouble.

"The night Red got infected." Crenel straightened, dropping the pretext of a casual conversation. "What made you so sure it wasn't the wolf?"

Penny shrugged. "It just didn't add up. The car we passed had to have been hit in daylight; the blood was too fresh. As far as Red has shown and all the mythological references we've found, werewolves are only active after dark and on a full moon." She raised a hand to forestall Crenel's objection. "I know the one we saw was maybe older, maybe has more control over when it shifts. It might play by different rules entirely. But punching a window in? Wolves don't have fists. And there's still the matter of the altar." She shook her head.

"You think someone was out there trying to summon something dead?" Crenel sounded curious rather than skeptical this time.

Instead of encouraging Penny, it threw her off. "I guess?

179

Or maybe it was a coven or some kind of demonic ritual. It could have been one of a million things. I just don't see how it can be related to the werewolf."

"You might be right about that." Crenel pushed himself off the desk and went to sit behind it, face tired and shoulders slumped. "Three more people have died out there, all attacked in their cars. And…"

He leaned back and lit a cigarette, much to Penny's alarm. She'd never seen him smoke inside the Academy.

"And what?" she demanded. "What else?"

"Someone came forward with new information about the accident you saw that day. The woman involved? She was seen with someone." He paused again to take another drag. "We can't be sure since the description was vague, but the artist she worked with was one of the best. We think Tobias was in the area."

"*Tobias?*" Penny had to force her fists to uncurl at his name. "What the hell is that slimy little pipsqueak doing out there?"

"Living on the beach, it sounds like." Crenel gave her a brief rundown. He'd been sighted talking to the victim at a gas station not long before her "accident." The attendant thought he might have been asking for money or a ride and got turned down. At least, that was her guess when he screamed "Bitch!" at her retreating car.

The security cameras hadn't caught his face, but the gas station attendant had given a decent-enough description, and a local beat cop had recognized him as one of Cannon Beach's local itinerant population, a guy who had only turned up a month or two ago.

"I can be there in a couple of hours." Penny rose, ready

to sprint out the door and catch the bastard who had almost killed her with a Kraken.

"Woah, *woah!*" Crenel grabbed her arm. "I called you in here to give you a heads-up, not to send you out on a manhunt, kid. This is above your paygrade. Whatever he's doing out there, he's not alone. Something is out in those woods, and dammed if I'm sending you out to deal with it."

He waited until Penny was seated before continuing. "We've got a whole team on it. They're armed to the eyeballs and good at what they do. Remember, Tobias is only human."

"So are they," Penny muttered. Still, Crenel had a point. The agents he had sent out to deal with this were far more qualified than she was. "So, what do you need me to do? There must be *something*, or you wouldn't have dragged me in here."

"What, can't a man admit he was wrong?" Crenel stubbed the cigarette out on an ancient ashtray. "But seeing as you offered… When are you working next?"

"Tomorrow night."

"I want you to ask around. See if anyone knows anything about a new entity down by the beach, or if they know anything about Tobias popping up. He's a bit of a celebrity in their circles, apparently." Crenel cocked an eyebrow, waiting for her response.

"That's just great." Penny stood, and this time, Crenel let her. "I'll do what I can, Agent Crenel. Thanks for keeping me in the loop."

Getting information out of the Mythers was harder than Penny expected. Though most were eager to assist—a violent entity slaughtering people was, after all, harming their cause—their ability to help was…well, lacking.

"Tobias, eh?" Gnorman—with a G thankyouverymuch, as he had informed Penny—sucked his thick white mustache. "I know a man named Arthur? Or what about Tamara? He might be the one you're looking for."

"Thanks, but I don't think so." Penny kicked herself for even thinking the gnome might be of help. Though he was of the less-homicidal variety than her previous encounter, the pointy-hatted little man had no understanding of gender, individuality or the passage of time.

I guess that's what you get when you're a garden ornament, Penny mused. Gnorman speared a bit of kale with a tiny fork.

"Ahh! What's that?" He pointed to a currant that had been hidden by the leaf.

"It's fruit, Gnorman. Not meat."

"But I'm a vegetarian!" He threw the cutlery down in disgust. "Fruit isn't a vegetable! I demand to see the manager!"

Penny sighed and motioned for Nat, the shift manager, to come over. "He's all yours," she said, giving the girl a sympathetic grimace.

"Gnorman, I've told you, fruit comes from plants. You're *allowed* to eat it!" Nat folded her arms, staring down her angry customer.

"Oh. Really?" He wrinkled his nose and sniffed the offending bit of food. "Isn't fruit usually…plumper?"

"It's dried," Nat explained.

She has the patience of a saint. Penny moved away, heading over to the bar where Paddy was chatting to Vila, Uriel, and the ghost of a little girl who apparently didn't have a name.

"And then," the girl was saying, her eyes large in her pale face, "she started burning sage. Can you believe it? That house was *my* home first, not hers!"

"Ye always have a home here, lass." Paddy slid a mug of ale toward the girl. She picked it up and sipped, screwing her face up.

"Paddy!" Penny grabbed his shoulder and hissed in his ear. "Mate, you just gave alcohol to a nine-year-old. Don't you know that's against the law?"

"She's a hundred and thirty-two," Paddy said, grinning. "Just because she's been dead for over a hundred of those years, it doesn't mean they don't count."

"Oh." Penny eyed the girl warily. "Well, regardless, if an inspector comes by, you might be in trouble."

"Aye, but if they call her a girl, they'll be sayin' she's human." Paddy cackled. "They'd be provin' me point without any effort on me own part!"

"And possibly get the bar shut down," Penny pointed out.

"Oh." Paddy's elation vanished, and he plucked the frothy beverage out of the little ghost's hands. "Maybe another time, lass."

"That doesn't seem fair." The child pouted but quickly cheered when Paddy leaned over the bar and snatched up a bowl of pretzels for her. "Yummy. I love those!"

Penny slid onto a barstool next to Paddy. "I'm on

break," she informed the leprechaun. "Don't start any trouble for the next fifteen, okay?"

"Me? Trouble?" Paddy's overplayed innocence didn't fool Penny for a moment. "Ah, fine. I'll just sit here and mind me own business. Only for a wee while, mind. Paddy can't be loungin' around for too long." He tossed a peanut in the air and caught it in his mouth, almost tumbling off his stool in the process.

"Good." Penny slid a photo toward the leprechaun.

He glanced down at it and shook his head. "I told ye, lass. I haven't seen the bastard since that day I met ye."

"Who is he?" Vila asked. She leaned over Paddy's shoulder to look. Then, in the blink of an eye, she shifted into her snake form. Black, glittering eyes examined the picture as a forked tongue flicked toward it. "Why do you ssseek him?"

"He's a guy who wants to summon some really bad shit," Penny explained. "He's trying to bring over Mythers who want to destroy the world. Paddy, I know you haven't seen him, but could you at least ask around for me? I haven't had any luck."

Paddy grimaced uncertainly, then looked at Vila.

Penny glanced at the shifter woman, only to find the snake was now a wolf.

"Get ye filthy paws off me bar, Vila!" Paddy snapped. "It's not a zoo."

Ignoring the leprechaun, Vila lifted her head. "Give me something of his. I will help you find him."

The wolf spoke in a low growl without moving her lips, but Penny understood the words perfectly.

"I don't have anything on me," she admitted. "But I can ask around. Will you be here tomorrow morning?"

The wolf ducked her head in a nod. "I will not capture this creature you seek. His blood on my teeth would undo what our kind have worked so hard for. Even seeking him out may make me anathema to others. But...I will find him for you."

"Thank you." Penny's chest tightened. She knew what Vila was risking to help her. Hunting a human could be interpreted as violating the alliance.

The wolf turned a tight circle on the bar and walked the length of it, claws tapping. When she reached the end, a graceful leap to the ground ended in her transformation back to the form of a slender woman in a simple white dress. She didn't look back, simply pushed the door open and stepped out into the cold streets of Portland.

"Hang on a hot minute." Penny frowned. "She just morphed into a human with a dress."

"Of course." The little ghost girl gave Penny a confused expression. "She is a god-shifter. She may choose her clothes and skin at any time."

"But she stripped down to give Red his lesson in shapeshifting. I thought that was because she *had* to."

"Strange one, that Vila." Paddy sipped his ale, then licked the frothy white mustache it left on his lip. "A bit of an exhibitionist, if ye haven't noticed." He picked up Tobias's picture and slipped it in his pocket with a sigh. "Fine. I'll ask around about ye wee villainous scumbag. But ye'll owe me!"

"Thanks, Paddy." Penny checked her watch. "Guess I'd

better get back to it. You may resume your troublemaking, leprechaun."

"May I also?" The little ghost beamed Penny a hopeful look.

Penny waved her off with a grin. "Sure, kid. Just don't make me salt you."

With a gleeful howl, the girl drifted to the ceiling and swooped a circle, moaning as she flew. "IIIIII am the ghooooost of Grace Mannnnooooorrrrr!" The spooky effect was somewhat marred by her occasional bursts of giggles. "IIII am heeeere to kiiiilllll yoooouuuuuu."

"And no killing!" Penny called to the mischievous spirit, who came to a halt with a child-like pout.

"Not even a little bit?" she asked.

"No!" Hiding her smile, Penny shook her head and went back to work.

CHAPTER SIXTEEN

V ila was indeed waiting for Penny the next morning. When Penny approached, the maiden's face fell.

"You did not find anything with his scent?"

Penny held out a scrap of paper. "I don't know. This was all I could get." It was a sheet torn from one of the copied versions of the Book of Thoth. Crenel had refused to let her access the original. "I'm not even sure he touched it, to be honest. This belonged to a girl he knew."

Vila plucked it from Penny's hand and ran it beneath her nose, inhaling deeply. "A girl, yes. Strong-minded. Broken once, but remade into iron."

Penny nodded. That described Felicity perfectly. "It's a bust, then?"

Vila inhaled again. "Perhaps not. I sense another. One full of hate and hated by the first. Did this girl wish your target to be ground into the dirt like the husk of a long-dead insect?" She asked the question as if she were asking about the color of shoes Tobias might be wearing.

"Uhh…yes. Or worse," Penny admitted.

Vila smiled and tucked the slip of paper beneath the bodice of her dress. Before the motion finished, she was back in her wolf form. "Wait."

The wolf tipped her nose up, gave a tentative sniff, and bounded down the street.

"Okay, then." Penny pushed the bar door open. The bar wasn't open yet, but she had spotted Paddy inside, nursing a drink at a table across from Joshua.

"I just don't understand," Paddy moaned. "Ye're givin' away our hard-earned coin!"

"_My_ hard-earned coin, you talkative gherkin." Joshua didn't look up as he spoke, simply continued to tap on his laptop. "My staff work a damn-sight harder than you do. Wages are _their_ hard-earned coin."

"You're not trying to stiff me outta my pay are you, Paddy?" Penny was already familiar with the leprechaun's whine about paying the bar staff. She didn't think it was malicious. The salty Myther really did seem to think money fell from trees, and that the workers could easily survive without being paid.

"Me pot grows smaller every day," he said dramatically. "Any more of this overtime nonsense and I'll run out of rainbows."

"That's bullshit, Paddy," Joshua said in a bored tone. "Your net worth is seventy-nine million. You're not running out of anything. Not even you could burn through that much on a weekend of hookers and blow."

"Seventy-what-now?" Penny's eyes nearly fell out of her head.

Joshua looked up. "Honestly, I'm not sure. It's solid gold, though. Seeing as I keep him fed, drunk, and out of the weather, it's not as if his expenses are unusually high. In fact, I've never seen him do more with his coin than show it off or toss it at homeless people. Well, people he thinks are homeless."

"Don't tell me that charming young lad with the ukulele wasn't in need of a good turn!" Paddy exclaimed. "Poor thing was wastin' away!"

Joshua rolled his eyes and leaned over to whisper to Penny. "He went to an Ed Sheeran concert and thought the kid was homeless and busking. On stage, in a sold-out theatre. With pyrotechnics!"

Penny covered her laugh with a hand.

"What brings you in this morning?" Joshua asked, finally folding away his laptop. "And do you want some coffee?"

'I can grab it," Penny said. She'd left the Academy without stopping by the dining hall. "Vila is doing me a favor. She said to wait here until she's done. I have no idea how long that will be."

"I'll do the coffee. No offense, but yours taste like wet goat." Joshua slid his chair back and went to the coffee machine. He expertly pulled two espressos and brought them back, along with a glass of whiskey for Paddy.

Penny accepted hers gratefully. She knew her coffee skills were… Lacking would be an understatement. Joshua had, however, made sure she knew her other skills were appreciated.

They chatted aimlessly until Joshua finished his book-keeping and excused himself, leaving Paddy and Penny alone.

Paddy slid Tobias's picture across the table, returning it

to Penny. "Sorry, lass. No one has seen him in person. I asked around the beach, though." He twiddled his whiskers for a moment before continuing, "Lass, things are brewin' out there. There was the wolf, aye, but somethin' else is makin' trouble. Enough trouble that a few of the friendlies in the region are movin' on. They don't wish to be associated with whatever is out there."

He scowled at Penny. "Are ye sure ye need to find the lad? If it's him causin' the ruckus out there, he could be summonin' the devil himself."

"Which is *exactly* why I need to find Tobias and stop him." Penny snatched the picture back. "I appreciate the warning, Paddy, but we can't just let him run loose. There's a whole community out there at risk. Do you think the government will support Mythers if Tobias keeps pulling crazy shit?"

"It's not as simple as that," Paddy said. "If some brave and handsome individual like meself goes out there and puts a stop to his shenanigans, that's another Myther killin' a human. If a hero who happens to look like one of them Greek gods, even though he's naught but a wee leprechaun, goes and puts down the creature he's summoned, that's Myther against Myther. That puts me alliance at risk, lass."

"I'm not asking any extraordinarily good-looking leprechauns to do either of those things," Penny pointed out, humoring the little green creature's high opinion of himself. "I just need a little information, that's all. So that I, a human, working for an agency that protects humans, can protect humans and Mythers alike." She didn't mention that Crenel had given her absolutely zero authority to hunt down Tobias or his new pet.

Paddy shrugged. "Like I said, I don't have any real information to go on. Just be careful, lass. I like havin' ye around."

Penny's heart swelled. Paddy wasn't one for compliments, and his words rang true. Before she could respond, though, something clattered against the glass window next to them.

"Oh, for... Ye stupid pigeon!" Paddy shook his fist, yelling at the dazed bird hopping in circles on the pavement outside. "I told ye, messages go through the door, ye blind disease-carrier."

The bird shook its head, then flapped into the air. It rounded the corner and slammed into the closed door of the bar, landing on the ground again.

"Ah, shit." Paddy stomped over and opened it, scooping the bird up with one hand and bringing it to the table.

Coo. The pigeon tilted its head and hopped to its feet. It stalked toward Penny, then dug under one wing with its beak, and pulled out a tiny scroll.

"That's new." Penny took the paper carefully, stroking the pigeon's head before pulling her arm back. "You ok, buddy? You gotta be more careful around windows, mate."

The bird nuzzled her hand, then made its way toward Paddy in awkward hopping steps. It perched on his whiskey glass and shat in it, then flew away, back out the open door.

"YE MITE-BITTEN BAG OF SNAKE FOOD!" Paddy slammed his fist on the table and looked into his glass morosely. "Next time it flies this way, I'll catch it and give it to Boots as a gift. What a wee prick."

Ignoring him, Penny unfurled the tiny message. It

folded out into a map the size of her palm, drawn in black ink. It showed the beach where the bonfire had been hosted, the trail through the woods, and the altar. Beyond it, marked on the edge of the mountain, was an X inside a narrow, upside-down V. In the bottom corner, Vila's name was signed.

"She found him!" Penny's eyes lit up. "I can't believe it!"

"What do you mean, four days?" Penny leaned over Crenel's desk, resisting the urge to punch it. "Do you know what Vila did to get that for you?"

"Believe me, I'm as pissed as you are." Crenel removed his glasses to rub his face. "We're just stretched thin right now."

"Then let *us* go!" Penny rounded back to her first response. But, even after forty minutes of arguing, Crenel wasn't having it.

"Not this time." Crenel slid his glasses back on. "Listen, kid, it's just too—"

Someone thumped on Crenel's door, not waiting for his response before throwing it open. Amelia burst in, hair wild, eyes rimmed with red. "Penny? There you are, I've been looking everywhere for you." She sucked in a shaky breath. "Red's gone."

Cisco stepped in behind her, face grim.

Penny pulled her friend into the room and grabbed her shoulders. "What? What do you mean, *gone*?"

"He's gone!" Amelia yanked her phone out and pressed

a couple of buttons. The buzz of a phone rang out on speaker, then the robotic voice of her voicemail service.

You have...one...saved message. Message received... today... ten-twenty-seven AM.

It beeped and Red's voice spoke, excitement thickening his accent. "I found it, sweet pea! It was in the cookie. I just have to go back to where it happened! I can cure it!" A car honked in the background as Penny listened, fear chilling her to the bones. "It's a long drive and tonight's the full moon, but I'll be back in the mornin', you'll see. And then I'll—" Amelia clicked the message off.

"What did the rest of it say?" Crenel demanded.

"Uhh, that bit wasn't fit for anyone else's ears." Amelia blushed. "Look, Red has gone on some stupid quest to cure himself, but he's going to wolf out as soon as the sun is down!"

"What cookie was he talking about?" Penny asked, mystified.

"He's gone back to that Chinese place a few times," Cisco suggested. "He's really got a vendetta against that cat. That, or he really likes the Kung-pow. Maybe he picked up an actual, real fortune cookie?"

"Any ideas?" Penny asked Amelia.

Amelia shrugged. "Damned if I know. But he said he's going back. Back where? Not to that stupid beach, I hope. I was cleaning sand out of my—"

"Oh, shit!" Penny grabbed Crenel's arm. "Please tell me you can get people there."

Crenel stared back, head slowly shaking. "I...can't. They didn't tell me what's going on, but our agents are working on something big. There's no one."

"No one but us." Penny dropped his wrist. "You *can't* keep us here. Not if Red is in danger."

"Are you sure that's where he's gone?" Crenel was already grabbing forms out of the stack of papers on his desk.

"He took his bedroll," Cisco confirmed.

"You'll need the big weapons bag. Audio and infra-red equipment, and anything else that might help you find him up in the hills." Crenel jotted down notes on the acquisition paperwork as he spoke. Without looking at it, he slid the tiny map back toward Penny, and she grabbed it. "Anything else?"

Penny bit her lip and sucked a breath in. "How about an Army tank?"

C renel couldn't get them an Army tank, but he got the next best thing. He tossed the keys of Mack's Jeep to Penny. "This will get you there safely. I'll help Cisco load up. Do you have everything?"

Penny glanced at the stacked crates and piled bags. She and Amelia had thrown clothes, weapons, and supplies together almost without thought. "The only thing we're missing is the kitchen sink." She gave him a brave smile and was rewarded with a proud grin in return.

"I'll be about fifteen minutes behind you." Crenel pointed to his Cadillac. "I'm doing my best to get us backup, so your first priority is to stay safe, okay?"

Penny nodded, elbowing a glowering Amelia. "Thank you, Crenel." Penny grabbed Amelia's arm. "It's a long drive. Let's grab coffee while the boys pack the car."

Amelia followed reluctantly. "If he thinks I'll stand by and let Red get hurt..."

"He doesn't think that at all," Penny reassured her. "But it's good to know we might have help."

"That depends on your definition of help." Amelia stopped mid-stride, pulling Penny back to look at her. "Penny, what if they treat Red as a threat?"

Amelia's reluctance to let Crenel get involved suddenly made sense. Penny grabbed her friend's shoulders. "Listen to me. Crenel is a friend. He's not going to let Red get hurt." She allowed herself a small smirk. "Besides, do you think March would ever let him get away with it?"

Amelia held her breath for a moment, searching her friend's face. She finally let out a deep sigh. "You're right. As long as Crenel is there, they won't cart him off like some kind of lab rat."

"Anyway, we're gonna get there first." Penny steered Amelia toward the dining hall. "Look, it's only an hour and a half drive, and it shouldn't get dark until around eight. That gives us loads of time to find Red and get him home before he turns on the puppy dog act."

Amelia glanced at her watch. "Five hours. Three of them driving. That gives us plenty of time to find him and convince him to come back with us. Right?"

"Sure." Penny winked. "Don't forget, we've got an escort who can flick on the lights and sirens if he needs to."

Amelia blew out another slow breath. "Ok. Let's do this."

The mid-week, late afternoon commute to the beach was smoother than the busy weekend. Penny had to watch her speed closely. Despite her promise to Amelia to make the trip as short as possible, the last thing they needed was a patrol car on their tail before Agent Crenel had caught up.

Speaking of which...

Penny turned the car radio down a little so she could be heard. "Amelia, can you send Crenel a text and see how far behind he is?"

"He just left. Fifteen minutes behind us, my ass," Amelia immediately said. "He's at least an hour behind. I've been harassing him since we left."

"What did he say about backup?" Cisco asked.

Amelia grunted. "Only that he's had no luck, but he won't give up."

"That doesn't matter," Penny said. "Look, I'd give my eyeteeth for a chance to hunt Tobias out here, but with luck, we won't run into him today. We just need to get in, find Red, and get out. Right?"

"Right," Cisco agreed.

"Sure, as long as I get to spend the trip back smacking him across the head for being so stupid," Amelia grumbled. "I swear to God, he's the biggest idiot I've ever seen."

That was the third time she had made that exact comment, peppered in among the words "dense," "moronic," and "downright mentally challenged."

Penny had let it slide, knowing that the words came from a place of concern. "We'll find him, Amelia. I promise."

Amelia tapped the armrest next to her impatiently and blew a stray lock of hair from her nose. "I know. I just wish it was done, you know? That I knew he was safe, and I could stop worrying."

Penny wished she could hug her friend, but had to make do with telling herself that of all the people she knew, Amelia was one of the strongest. Red would be okay, and so would Amelia.

Glancing in the rear mirror, Penny smiled to see Boots nudge Amelia's chin comfortingly.

"How far to go?" Amelia asked.

"Twenty miles, maybe?" Penny squinted into the afternoon sun. "Not far."

"Do we have a plan for when we get there?" Cisco asked.

"He got the scratch when we took the beast down in the woods," Penny said. She chewed her lip. "Makes sense that's where he'd be."

"Are you thinking something else?" Ever observant, Cisco flashed her a look.

Penny shrugged. "I just thought… that car we saw is just up ahead. I know it'll chew a bit of time, but I feel like we should check it out on the way past." She lifted her eyes to look in the mirror, tilting her head so she could see Amelia. Beside her friend, Boots had her head pressed flat against the window. *She's thinking the same thing I am.*

Still, this wasn't a choice Penny could make alone. "Only if everyone agrees, though."

"No, that makes sense," Amelia said. "Red's message was too cryptic, yet another reason he needs a smack across the head. Did it begin when he contracted the lycanthropy, or when the adventure started? Hell, maybe he's gone to visit his hometown, back in Ireland." Amelia scowled.

Penny snorted. "You know what he meant. But, yeah. I just think there is a chance that he stopped here, too." She didn't add that if they found evidence of Tobias out there or something that pointed to him, she'd be ecstatic. That wasn't her goal, just a nice bonus if they came across it.

The wreck was only a few minutes ahead. When Penny

pulled the Jeep over on the road shoulder, there was little left apart from some skid marks on the road and a loose strip of police tape still staked into the ground. Boots was the first to slither out, tongue flickering in and out curiously.

Penny stepped out of the Jeep and winced when she realized the ground was soft with mud. "Gross." It had rained two days earlier back at the Academy, but this seemed more recent despite the clear blue sky above.

"At least you have sensible shoes on," Amelia groaned as her own shoes sank almost an inch deep. "Boots, how are you still clean?"

The serpent gave a haughty cough and continued toward the site of the wreck, sliding over the wet soil without attracting any of it.

"That's the first time I've heard you call these old things anything but... well, old." Penny took a long, tenuous stride out of the puddle she had parked in and walked over to a spot where deep ruts were torn in the patchy roadside grass. "I think this is where it was parked. Watch out, Boots. There's glass everywhere."

The tiny jagged cubes glittered, crunching under Penny's hard soles as she stomped over them, eyes on the ground. For the most part, the accident had been cleared up, but dark stains still marked the ground, and several trees had been damaged.

Cisco ran his fingers along one gouged trunk while Boots rose her head to examine it. "I don't think a car did that."

"Doesn't look werewolfish, either." Amelia wrapped her arms around her middle, hugging herself tightly. "I mean.

Does it? I guess I don't really know what a werewolf attack would look like."

Penny frowned. "Wolves have claws and teeth. This looks… not like that." She wedged the flat of her hand in the jagged cut. "There's no way teeth did this, and it's the wrong shape for claws."

"One giant claw, maybe?" Cisco held up his forefinger, crooked over like a talon. He swung it toward the tree.

"Yeah, a one-fingered wolf. Makes total sense." Penny rolled her eyes at his injured expression. "Seriously, though, I don't think it was a wolf. Or a werewolf. It just doesn't look *right*."

Penny checked the other trees. Each one was damaged in a different way. One had cracked, its thick trunk flattened on one side and splintered on the other. Flakes of red paint were embedded into the bark.

"Car," Cisco said decisively. "Our vic must have slammed her car into this one."

"Our 'vic?'" Penny asked. "Mate, were you up all night watching *Law and Order again*?"

"No!" Cisco looked away. "It was *Brooklyn Nine-Nine*."

"Even better." Amelia groaned. "Seriously, Cisco, this is important!"

"Hey, I'm trying, okay? I want to find Red as much as you guys do." He glanced at the damage that surrounded them. "I'd really like to know what did this, though."

Boots let out a sudden hiss, raising her upper body into the air for attention.

Penny jogged over. "Guys? Look!" They were at the edge of the crash site, close to the wooded area beyond. She pointed one finger at a crisp boot print in the dirt.

"Boots, you're amazing. That's Red's, all right." Cisco stepped away, lining up the angle of the boot. "I've cleaned up that muddy print more times than I'd like to admit. The guy is getting a doormat and a mop for his birthday, I swear."

"The second one is here," Penny guessed, pointing at a grassier spot where a heel had sunk into some exposed soil at one edge. She followed the footprints for a few feet, then looped back around. "Dead end. It looks like he looked around and then left." She looked at Boots for confirmation, but the serpent just circled the friends, tail twitching nervously.

They poked around a little while longer but didn't find anything of interest. Penny squinted at the dropping sun. "We should go. He's not here. He probably went back to where it happened."

She didn't elaborate on what *it* was. None of them needed the reminder that a werewolf had lurked in the nearby forest, or that they'd found an altar there too.

Who knows what else is out there. Penny shook off the chill that ran down her back. *It doesn't matter what's out there. Whatever it is, we can face it. For Red.*

"You're crapping your pants too, aren't you?" Amelia asked, giving Penny a tight grin.

"Was it that obvious?" Penny linked her arm through her friend's. "It doesn't matter, though. Creepy stick dolls and abandoned altars are no match for us. Right?"

A branch squeaked in the breeze, and something scurried through the dead leaves scattered over the ground. Boots rose in a defensive posture, then darted over to wrap around Penny's leg.

"Right!" Amelia squeaked. She glanced back with wide eyes. "But that doesn't mean we can't run!"

It was all Penny needed. She sprinted for the car and threw herself inside, only turning to peer out the window once Amelia was safe too. Cisco sauntered back with a smirk on his face.

"Really?" he called. "You ran? You two can face a giant wolf, but one little rat rustling a few leaves sends you running like gir—"

"You can say girls, Cisco," Penny informed him. "We ran like girls. Swiftly. Gracefully, even. Like girls." She sat back in her seat and folded her arms. "And we weren't scared. We were…" Her voice trailed off as she wracked her brain for an excuse.

"We were having a race," Amelia said. "To keep our reflexes up. That's all."

"*Suuure.*" Cisco slid into the driver's seat and held out a hand for the car keys.

Penny gave a silent curse. She had thrown herself into the passenger seat and was now stuck with letting Cisco drive. Unless, of course, she admitted why she'd jumped in without thinking. As if.

She tossed him the keys and buckled her belt. "Thanks. I needed the break."

"Uh-huh." Still wearing his shit-eating grin, Cisco started the Jeep and pulled back onto the highway. "You keep telling yourself that. Meanwhile, if we meet an actual monster out there, I'll just ask it to wait until you two finish 'honing your reflexes' before we fight it."

Unable to form a reasonable response, Penny punched

Cisco's arm. Not hard—after all, he had a point—but hard enough to get her point across.

"Fine, I'll drop it." Cisco turned his head to glance out the window but not enough to obscure his low mutter. "Pussies."

She punched him again. "We are not!"

"Not what?" Amelia demanded from the back seat.

Cisco chuckled then flinched when Penny drew her fist back again. "Okay, Okay! you're not pussies!"

"You're *such* a child, Cisco." Amelia spoke in a tone of well-worn patience. "Honestly."

"Me, a child?" Cisco yanked the mirror so he could glare at Amelia.

"Just concentrate on driving, please?" Penny shot at Cisco.

Scoffing, Cisco turned his attention back to the road. "I'm an excellent driver, thank you."

The road curved and he nudged the wheel, the scatter of houses that passed vanishing in the rearview mirror as the ocean came into view.

"How far is the rec site?" Amelia asked, leaning forward.

"Not far." Cisco glanced at the GPS. "Less than a mile."

"About a click," Penny said at the same time. Her eyes rose to meet Cisco's, a smile on her lips.

Bang.

The car jerked to a stop, momentum halted so abruptly that the rear wheels lifted and smashed back down.

The impact sent Penny lurching forward, seatbelt pinning her back like a chain. The windshield shattered, and someone screamed as an air-filled pillow slammed into Penny's face.

CHAPTER EIGHTEEN

Penny's lungs strained, trying to suck air into her aching chest, thwarted by a stunned diaphragm. After what seemed an eternity, it worked. Gasping, she batted away the deflating airbag and fumbled for the clasp of her seatbelt.

"Boots! Cisco?" she croaked. "Amelia?" Boots wriggled onto Penny's lap, flicking her slender tongue at Penny's face as if tasting for blood. Penny touched a bump on her head. Her fingers came back smudged with red.

"I'm okay," Amelia said. "What the fuck happened?"

"Ran into something." Cisco sounded strained but managed a rueful grin. "My bad, I guess. Damned if I know what it was, though. It ran out on the road before I could stop."

Penny reached for her door latch, heart climbing into her throat when she pushed and nothing happened. "My door is stuck."

"Let me try." Amelia climbed out and came to stand by Penny's door. She glanced at the front of the car and paled, but quickly turned her attention back to Penny. "It's just a bit banged up."

Penny ushered Boots out of the way, then used her legs to shove the door as Amelia pulled. It jerked open with a *thunk*. "Thanks."

Cisco managed to shoulder his own door open, and together, they went to examine the damage.

"Holy hell." Penny reached out a tentative hand to touch the wedged indent. It was a foot deep and sharply curved. Images of the damaged tree filled Penny's mind, and although she shook them away, her anxiety remained.

"There's nothing here." Amelia glanced around with a worried frown. "What did we hit?"

"Something ran off the road after it happened." Cisco had one hand pressed to the side of his neck and stood with his weight on one foot. "A shadow. I only caught it out of the corner of my eye."

"Are you okay?" Penny took Cisco's hand, gently pulling it away to reveal an angry bruise that was beginning to swell where his seatbelt had grazed his skin. "What's wrong with your foot?"

Cisco winced. "My knee. It's a little banged up, but nothing major. Were either of you hurt?"

Amelia's fingers touched the side of her head. "Just a bruise."

Penny took a moment to run through a mental check. *Arms, legs, fingers, toes. Head's okay. I mean, it can't get any uglier.* "My chest hurts, but other than that, just a few bumps and scrapes."

"Well, we can't stay here. I don't know what we hit, but I'd kind of like to keep it that way." After a wary glance at the nearby forest, Cisco walked to the back of the Jeep and popped the trunk. "Guess we'd better start walking. The question is, which direction are we headed?"

"What?" Amelia stepped back. "No, idiot. We call for help."

Cisco didn't seem upset at Amelia's snapped reply. "Check your phone. If you've got reception, call away. But I've got nothing, and even if we do get help, it'll be a couple of hours away."

Penny yanked her phone out and saw he was right. "Damn."

Amelia groaned. "I *hate* it when he's right." She looked around expectantly, then gestured impatiently at Penny. "Come on, you're the smart one. What do we do?"

Penny snorted. "Me? Smart? That's a new one." She peered along the deserted road, then checked her watch. "Look, we still have a couple of hours left before the sun goes down. It'll take us what, thirty minutes to get to the recreation site? I say we head that way. Agent Crenel should get there around the same time we do, allowing for the stop we made earlier. He'll see the car and stop. We can leave a note to tell him where we went."

"What about our gear?" Cisco pointed to the trunk of the car. "There's no *way* we can carry all of that."

Penny shrugged. "Then we take what we absolutely need, lock the rest up, and we go. Come on, guys. We need to find Red. With a bit of luck, we can drag him out right when secret agent superhero turns up looking for us. We get him home before sundown, stick him in a safe place, and kill him in the morning for being such an idiot."

Boots gave a nervous hiss and slithered a few feet down

the road, signaling her agreement to move on. When no one moved to join her, she returned and head-butted Cisco's ankle, trying to get him to move.

"I get it." Cisco raised his hands in defeat. "I'm outnumbered. I'd still feel better if someone knew where we were going." Despite his hesitation, Cisco popped the trunk. He started rifling through their equipment, pulling out three utility belts, and reorganizing the contents of several bags.

Penny glanced at her phone one more time. *Nothing.* She tapped out a text anyway, addressing it to Agent Crenel.

Wrote off the car but we are fine. Heading up to the rec site on foot to look for Red. Left you a note. Don't take too long.

Penny tapped Send, frowning when the phone pinged back a red exclamation mark and a line saying **Message undeliverable**. *Hopefully, it'll get through if we hit a good spot.*

Penny insisted on taking the backpack, letting Cisco shoulder the duffel bag. "The straps will rub your neck, but at least you can carry that on your good side," she told him.

Cisco grinned. "You're saying I have a good side?"

"Only if the light isn't great." Penny winked as she strapped her utility belt on and stuffed it with the items she couldn't fit in her bag. They would need to carry as much as they could without it slowing them down.

Amelia scribbled a note on some bright yellow paper filched from one of Penny's packs. She taped it to the inside of the windshield with adhesive tape from the first aid kit. "There is no way he'll miss that. Are we ready?"

"Let's go." Without waiting for her friends, Penny set off down the road. Cisco quickly caught up to walk beside her, and the steady crunch of Amelia's footsteps announced her presence behind them.

"Are you sure this is a good idea?" Cisco asked quietly.

"Do you have a better one?" Penny adjusted the strap over her left shoulder. "Sorry. I know what you mean, though. What in the hells do you think we hit?"

"Honestly?" Cisco glanced back toward Amelia, then dropped his voice further. "We hit something hard, something big enough to bring us to a dead stop. Something strong enough to scurry away after the impact. Anything with that kind of strength could easily have busted up that car we saw and smashed into the trees."

A sense of dread that Penny had been trying to ignore blossomed in her gut. "You think we're walking into a giant trap." It wasn't a question.

"Not necessarily. I mean, maybe we scared it off." Cisco shook his head. "If it was going to attack us, it probably would have done it right away. Still, I don't know. Maybe *I'm* the pussy."

"You know what they say—you're not paranoid if someone is really out to get you." Penny gave a low chuckle. "Look, we're traipsing through the woods a couple of hours before sundown. Last time we were here, someone let a werewolf loose. We *know* Tobias is likely out here working around, and God only knows who or what he's been trying to summon. I think a little fear of this situation is pretty healthy."

"But?" Amelia asked.

This time it was Penny who glanced back at Amelia. She sighed. "But we can't leave Red out here alone.

Anyway, Boots wouldn't lead us astray. She has excellent intuition about this sort of thing."

"What if we can't find him?" Amelia's voice was quiet, almost snatched away by the gentle breeze that brushed Penny's face.

"We will." Penny stopped walking long enough to drop back next to her friend. She wrapped a comforting arm around Amelia's shoulders. "I'm sure of it."

It took the trio half an hour to arrive at the Arcadia recreation site. Despite the cool weather, a thin sheen of sweat chilled Penny's skin, and she shivered when they stopped moving. She cast a concerned eye at the sun, already dropping ominously low in the sky.

"Red?" Cisco cupped his hands around his mouth and let out a loud yell. "Red! Are you out here?"

They waited in silence for a moment, then Penny shrugged off her backpack and set it on the ground. "Looks like we're doing this the hard way. I don't want to be carrying all this with us. If we're going into the forest, we will need to be able to maneuver quickly."

"Are you thinking we should stash the bags somewhere?" Cisco asked.

Penny nodded. "While we go for a quick scout around. We can come back for them if we need to."

"What about our ride home?" Amelia had already set her knapsack down. She pulled out a flashlight and a small first aid kit, slipping the first into a loop on her belt and clipping the second to a spare carabiner. "Finding Red is one thing. We also have to get him home before nightfall, remember?"

"Then we better not waste any time. Let's take some flares." Cisco nodded toward the sheltered picnic area. "We can leave another note here, explaining what we're doing."

"Are you sure that's safe?" Penny kicked herself for not thinking of it back at the car. "What if the wrong person sees where we're going? If something is after us..."

"If there is, we will just have to hope it can't read." Amelia scribbled a second note while Penny and Cisco stocked up on supplies. She nodded at the bags. 'We can't just leave those lying around. Any ideas?"

Cisco wandered over to the nearby restrooms. He disappeared around the corner, reappearing moments later with a look of determination. "Here, there's a supplies room we can use."

Penny picked up her bag and followed him around the small building. She eyed the gleaming padlock holding the door closed. "I'm no clairvoyant, but I foresee some destruction of public property in your near future, Cisco."

He shook off her concern. "We can come back out and replace it. Right now, a broken padlock is pretty low on my list of concerns. Can you imagine what would happen if some drunk teenager found our stuff?"

Can't argue with that. Penny passed Cisco her backpack, keeping only the empty bag she used for hauling her scaled friend around. She grabbed Amelia's pack too as she appeared around the corner.

Once they were stored, Cisco secured the door with a thick plastic zip tie. "It's not perfect, but it will stop anyone from opening it accidentally."

Penny bit her lip and wiped her sweaty palms on her jeans. "Looks like we are done here. Let's go, team." A tug at her ankle held her back, and she looked down. "What, you're sick of walking?"

Boots ducked her head in a nod, and at Penny's gesture, rose up to climb into her bag. When Penny slung it back over her shoulder, Boots popped her head out to rest it on Penny's shoulder.

"You can be our lookout," Penny said. Boots wriggled unhappily. "What, you thought I'd let you sleep on the job? Not likely!"

They headed toward the road and crossed it unhindered. Penny wasn't sure if she was grateful for the lack of people. On the one hand, if something happened, they wouldn't have to worry about innocent people getting hurt. On the other...

It's not like Tobias would be held back by a crowd, she reminded herself. *If anything, he would be drawn by it. Let's hope that means he's not here.*

The sun had dipped behind the hills, casting a shadow that sucked the last of the warmth from the day. "Let's pick up the pace," Penny said. "We're in a hurry, but also, I'm freezing my ass off."

"You're such an Aussie," Cisco teased. He ignored Boots' offended hiss. "What would happen if you went somewhere that was actually cold? You'd freeze to death!"

"It's not my fault you lot can't appreciate a nice, sunny, forty-five-degree day." Penny pushed a branch out of her way. When something tickled her hand, she snatched it back with a yelp as Boots gave a startled hiss. "Was that a spider?"

"What is it?" Cisco took a quick step toward her, then snatched the dangling bundle of sticks that had scared her.

Penny took one look at the five-pointed shape bound with red twine and cursed. "Never thought I'd say this, but I would have preferred a huntsman."

"Pentacles don't jump at you. At least we're on the right track." Amelia seemed undaunted by the makeshift pentacle. "We must have missed those last time, but if my guess is right, those creepy dolls are just ahead."

Unfortunately, Amelia's guess *was* right. As the trees thinned, Penny was easily able to spot at least two dozen tiny figures dangling from red nooses in the branches above. Somehow, they seemed even creepier in the fading light than they had in the darkness.

"We should yell again." Cisco's face said the opposite of his words. "Shouldn't we?"

"Let's not." Penny pushed ahead, arguing with the knot of terror in her stomach. *What are you so afraid of? It's just some idiot who's watched the* Blair Witch Project *too many times. Just because that stupid movie scared the pants off of you, it doesn't mean anything bad is going to happen out here.*

"You know," Amelia said, her voice loud in the quiet forest. "Those stick dolls scare me more than the Kraken did. That makes no sense, right?"

"Would you stop reading my mind?" Penny mustered up a shaky grin. "I swear to God, I'm never watching a horror movie ever again."

"They're just sticks." Cisco only sounded marginally more comfortable than the girls. "They can't hurt us. We'd better watch out, though. If Tobias has been lurking around here, who knows what kind of creepy shit he's been up to."

"Thank you *so* much for reminding us that there are plenty of things to be terrified of out here," Amelia said. She drew the handgun from her belt and raised it carefully. "The altar was just ahead. Be careful, guys."

Boots dropped herself to the ground, tail trembling as she nosed the scattered leaves. Penny stepped into the clearing, stomach clenched against a flutter of nerves and adrenalin. She skirted the edge before walking over to the altar. "Guys?" she whispered. "I think Red was here."

"What makes you say that?" Cisco asked.

Penny held up a plastic card. "This is his Academy ID." She brushed off the dirt and passed it to Cisco. "Do you think he dropped it?"

Cisco shook his head. "No way. He keeps it tucked in the back of his wallet. He must have left it on purpose."

Amelia nodded in agreement. "Cisco's right. He couldn't have dropped it without realizing."

Leaves rustled, and Penny spotted Boots headed toward a tree at the clearing's edge.

"Look!" Cisco pointed above the snake. A branch had snapped, clinging crookedly to the trunk by a splintered thread. He darted a glance around. "Let's check it out."

Penny held the branch back in place, then wiggled it. The wood was still soft and damp. "Still fresh. Whatever broke it was going in this direction." She examined the forest floor where Boots had brushed aside the dead foliage to reveal hard, dry dirt. "Guys? I think there's a trail!"

Amelia held back. "It's just over two hours until

sundown. We need to figure out what we're gonna do if we don't find him soon."

"Keep looking," Cisco answered immediately. "It's okay, Amelia. We won't give up."

Amelia shook her head resolutely. "That's just dumb. What if we get lost, or pass straight by him? Or he wolfs out in the car on the way back? We can't risk that." She wrapped her arms around herself. "We need a plan."

"You think we should leave him to fend for himself?" The idea made sense, but Penny felt uneasy about it. "I guess he could fight off most stuff in wolf form, but I don't think I could just abandon him out here."

"I'm not saying we should leave, but maybe we should put a time limit on our search. If we don't find anything before then, we head back and look for Crenel." Amelia's posture relaxed as she talked it through. "He'll know how far away our backup is, and he can help us search. And if we find Red and he turns—"

"They'll be able to keep him safe," Penny finished for her. "Damn. That's a good plan."

"How long?" Cisco glanced at the woods behind him. "I don't want to give up yet."

"An hour," Amelia said firmly. "As long as we don't get lost, we should be able to head back faster than we're searching. That should give us time to get back before it gets too dark."

And before the wolf starts hunting. Penny wondered if the same thought had crossed Amelia's mind.

Cisco pressed a few buttons on his watch. "Timer set. Let's go." He turned his back on Penny and Amelia and strode into the trees.

"Wait for us!" Amelia lunged to follow him, leaving Penny to follow behind.

The trail was faint, nothing more than a worn track through the woods where the leaf litter was scattered and the grass was thinner. They lost their way several times, backtracking to search for a more obvious route.

Penny counted the minutes as they walked, sighing with relief as the uphill trek began to slope back down. Soon, shadows encased them as the track became a dry trench carved deep into the hill.

Cisco glanced up nervously. "We're getting pretty deep in here. And it's tight."

He was right. The group had to walk single file through the narrow gorge. "What if it's a trap?"

Penny slowed behind him. "Amelia? What do you think?"

Amelia rubbed her arms. "I don't know. Boots? What is it?"

The serpent had risen to her full height, balancing on her tail like a stretched out spring. She tasted the air, then bared her teeth in an angry hiss.

"Okay, time to go back," Cisco said. Before he could nudge Penny back along the trail, though, a weak cry trembled through the air.

"What was that?" Penny whispered. Goosebumps tickled the back of her neck as it came again.

"Help!"

"Red?" Cisco's uncertainty was written all over his face.

"Does it matter?" Amelia bit her lip, then continued, "Whoever that is, we can't just leave them there."

"You're right." Penny put her hand down to touch

Boots' head. The serpent butted her back forcefully. "It's probably a trap, and even if it isn't, if someone is out here and needs help…"

"There's no one else for miles." Cisco blew out a sharp breath, then turned on his heel. "Stay quiet. Keep your eyes up and your weapons out."

Penny drew the handgun from her belt. It felt small in her hand, inadequate as she imagined what kind of beast could sustain that kind of impact with their car and survive.

Boots, meanwhile, wasn't willing to trust Cisco at the front of the pack. She twisted between his feet, almost tripping him as she moved ahead, rainbow shimmer dulled by the deep shadows and dropping light.

Another cry for help rang out, this time closer. Cisco slowed, forcing Penny and Amelia to do the same. At a sharp hiss, he stopped completely.

Penny edged around in time to see Boots head-butt him firmly, trying to push him back.

Instead, Cisco ducked low and peeked around a sharp corner, then drew back.

"What did you see?" Penny itched to look as well but resisted the urge.

One of the lessons Quaid had taught the students was that more movement meant more chance of discovery. One person could sneak into a house with only a moderate risk. Two? It didn't just double the chance of discovery, it exploded it. The more people involved, the bigger the risk that one of them would give the game away.

"Dead end," Cisco murmured. "Someone on the ground. A guy, I think, but dark hair. It's definitely not Red."

"Dead?" Penny whispered.

Cisco gave a quick shake of his head. "Alive, but he didn't look like he was in great shape."

"What do we do?" Amelia had crept up but stayed far enough back to stay hidden.

"Stay quiet," Cisco whispered. "We need to—" He was interrupted by a shrill beep. "Shit!" He fumbled in his pocket and pulled out his phone, jabbing the screen with a finger repeatedly as he tried to silence the timer.

Penny yanked it out of his hand, tapped the 'stop' icon, and passed it back.

"Gee, do you think anyone heard?" Cisco muttered.

"Is anyone there?" The voice that called out wasn't Red's, but it tugged at Penny's memory. "Hello? Please, I'm hurt. You need to help me!"

"You gotta be fucking kidding me." Unwilling to believe the piteous whine could possibly belong to who she thought it did, Penny stood and stalked around the corner, gun trained on the slumped figure across from her. "*Corey?* What in all the hells are you doing here?"

Penny eyed her former classmate. His dirt-smudged face looked up from the deepening shadows, blood dripping down one cheek from a nasty scratch.

"Corey? You mean that douchebag who got himself kicked out of the Academy?" Amelia appeared beside her. "Oh, it *is* the douchebag. What's up, Corey?"

"Fuck you," he snarled.

Penny wagged a finger. "That's no way to speak to your would-be rescuers. We could just go home, you know."

"No!" His eyes darted around anxiously. "You can't leave me here. I was attacked!"

"By what?" Penny's dismay at seeing someone she disliked so intensely was already fading into worry. *What possible reason could he have for being out here?*

"I don't know. I was at that park near the beach when something big came outta nowhere. It hit me over the back of my head, and I woke up here." He grimaced and pointed to his left foot. "I think I've broken my ankle. I can't walk."

Penny narrowed her eyes, then yanked Amelia and Cisco back around the corner. Boots stayed where she was, fangs bared as she watched Corey with wary eyes.

"If he was at the rec area, how did he get there?" Penny asked. "We didn't see any other cars."

"Something definitely smells funny," Cisco admitted. "But we can't just leave him there. Not if he's really injured."

Amelia hesitated, then nodded. "We're out of time to find Red anyway. As much as I hate Corey, I'd feel at least a little bad if we left him here to die." She grinned. "Besides, if we ever run into him again, we can lord it over him. That alone will be worth it."

Cisco shook his head. "I don't like it." He held up a hand to forestall Penny's protest. "I know, I know. We have to help him. But I don't have to like it. It's too convenient."

"A broken ankle is convenient?" Amelia *tsked*. "I'd hate to see your idea of *in*convenient."

Cisco scowled. "You know what I mean. Just be careful. Keep your eyes open and be prepared to move fast."

"We know." Penny squeezed Cisco's elbow for reassurance, then holstered her gun and stepped back out into the closed-off gorge. "Corey? We're going to help you. Just stay calm."

Corey's face twisted up. "Just don't bring that reptile anywhere near me."

Boots responded with an angry hiss. She darted her head forward, making Corey flinch back.

"Boots!" Penny turned to the snake so that Corey wouldn't see her smothered grin. "That was rude. Go and stand in the corner, young lady." She waved Boots away.

Boots ducked her head and slithered off, but Penny wasn't convinced by the silent apology. She let it rest, though. "I've only got a basic first aid kit with me," she explained to Corey. "But I can bandage your ankle and we can carry you out, okay?"

Corey nodded. Sweat beaded on his forehead despite the chill in the air and he grabbed Penny's arm, pulling her closer. "It really hurts," he said.

Penny nodded as she shook loose his tight grip. "Sure. I'll be careful." She knelt and carefully rolled up the hem of his jeans. Frowning, she bent down for a better look. "Corey? I don't see—"

A soft click froze the blood in her veins. Her eyes darted up to look directly into the barrel of the gun Corey had pointed at her face.

Penny swallowed. "Corey, I'm going to raise my hands, okay?" She lifted them slowly, forcing her eyes to stay on his rather than search for her friends.

"You dumb bitch," he said with a coarse laugh. "As if I'd need help from *you*."

"Corey, come on, man. You thought we were unarmed?" Cisco asked.

Penny finally dropped her gaze and glanced at Cisco, whose gun was pointed at Corey.

Corey laughed again. "Come on, Cisco," he imitated. "You thought I was *alone*?"

A shadow made Penny's breath catch. Tobias stepped out from behind Cisco. "Well, well, well. Didn't we get lucky today?"

CHAPTER NINETEEN

Tobias finished zip-tying Cisco's hands, then shoved him to the ground next to Penny and Amelia. "Wait here," he said to Corey. "I'll go get that Irish bastard. Together, they should make a big enough sacrifice to give us full control over our boy."

Penny would have asked questions, but she had already come to the conclusion that she didn't want the answers. *Just as well*, she decided. *My teeth are chattering too hard to talk anyway.*

The cold had set in as the sun dropped. It wasn't yet night time, but purple streaks in the sky and heavy shadows in the gorge had brought with them a bone-deep chill that her thin jacket couldn't hold off.

Amelia had no such trouble. "Sacrifice for what? Where's Red? Tell me what you did to him, you sadistic prick."

Tobias turned a cold smile on her. "You know, you would have been much happier with me. It's a pity your friends ruined that. You might have even lived past today."

Unimpressed, Amelia gave an unladylike snort. "Whatever you say, Romeo."

Tobias's eyes burned with hate, his jaw pulsing with anger. "I'll make sure you die one at a time. You can go last. Maybe watching your friends be torn to shreds will fix your attitude."

"Yeah. It probably won't." Amelia turned big eyes his way. "Assholes like you just bring out the *worst* in me."

Tobias sucked in a breath and stalked over to Corey, who sat against a stray fallen rock fiddling with his gun.

"You're sure it'll work?" Corey asked the older man.

Tobias sneered. "What, you're scared? I thought more of you."

"No!" Corey ground his teeth. "But you said he'd obey us."

Tobias shook his head. "I said he'd obey us once the rituals were complete, you idiot. We still need two more victims to complete them."

"What do we do with the other two?" Corey demanded.

Tobias smiled, a cold, glittering grin that sliced over Penny and her friends. "Once he's under our control, we can afford to let him play with them for a little. Until he kills them, too."

Tobias left. Corey cocked his weapon at Amelia and made the soft sound of a gunshot.

"You're gonna shoot yourself in the dick if you keep playing with that," Amelia called.

Penny shushed her. "Corey, you don't have to do this," she pleaded. "Tobias won't keep you safe. He's pure evil. You have no idea what you're getting yourself into."

"Why, because I didn't finish at that stupid school?"

Corey barked a laugh. "*You* have no idea. Those teachers are dumb. They think their books have all the answers, but they haven't seen what's out here."

"How would he know what's in any book," Amelia whispered loudly. "Can he even read?"

"Amelia, shut up!" Penny hissed.

"Corey, let us go," Cisco chimed in. "You're going to get yourself hurt. Or worse."

Corey lifted his hand, the gun dangling off one finger by the trigger. "Who has the weapon, dipshit? What, you think your mama's gonna run in here and give me a detention for being mean to you?"

Cisco muttered something under his breath, then leaned his head back to whisper to Penny. "He's not gonna give in."

"I can't believe my luck," Corey crowed, his voice cracking with joy. "When I found Tobias, he promised I'd be able to get back at you someday. But then you just stumble on in, looking for your idiot friend! He's dead, by the way. Or he will be soon."

"I know," Penny ignored Corey, giving Cisco a sad look. "But we had to give him the chance."

"Shut up!" Corey stood, brandishing the weapon. "Stop whispering. Bandage Man will be here soon. I can't wait until he destroys you."

"Do it," Penny called.

"Do what?" Corey snapped. "He's not *here* yet. I told you that."

Penny laughed. "I wasn't talking to you."

It was unlikely that Corey heard her response. Indeed, the high pitched scream he let out was enough to deafen

Penny as the six-foot-long serpent launched herself from the shadows and buried her teeth in their captor's arm.

The gun fell, skidding across the dirt. Corey punched at Boots' head but she didn't let go, twisting her body to wrap around his arm as her fangs kneaded deeper into his flesh.

Cisco slammed his body into the dirt on top of the fallen weapon.

"Cisco, you idiot, you'll shoot yourself!" Penny snapped. She contorted her body to bring her hands around to her front.

Corey's screams rose to a fever pitch as he finally managed to dislodge Boots, prying her head up and flinging her to the ground. She struck again, this time a sharp, fast snap at his leg.

Corey threw himself behind the rock. He rose, brandishing an old branch, and swung it at Boots.

"Don't you dare!" Penny ran, legs pumping, and threw herself at him. Her hands might be tied, but her shoulder slammed into his chest, and they fell to the ground.

Corey grabbed at her hair and caught her face, but Penny rolled away, landing a solid kick into Corey's midriff.

She twisted back and pinned him down. "You had the option to do this the easy way," she grunted. "But no, you had to be an asshole."

Corey spat at her. He missed, the saliva covering his own face instead.

"Wow, Corey, that's *so* attractive." Amelia looked down, pointing Corey's weapon at him. "You okay, Penny?"

Penny nodded. "Sure. I'm starting to regret giving him a

chance to redeem himself, though. He really is a jerk down to his bones, isn't he?"

"Got it!" Cisco held up his hands, zip-tie dangling from one and a small knife in the other. "Now we just have to—" His voice fell away, jaw dropping as his eyes bulged.

Penny glanced back, barely catching a rush of movement from the corner of her eye.

"Penny! Catch!" Penny looked up at the urgency in Cisco's voice as the folded blade spun toward her. She reached out to catch it. Before her fingers could curl around it, a rough hand grabbed her hair, yanking her back with a wordless roar. The blade tumbled to the ground, forgotten.

Hot, wet breath panted against Penny's neck as loose fabric tickled her collarbone.

Amelia pointed the gun toward Penny, slowly backing away. "Let her go!"

Her eyes were wide and scared. Penny's brain scrambled to make sense of what was happening. All she knew was that whatever had her, it wasn't Corey.

He had scrambled back, his eyes darting toward the only exit from the gorge.

The gun fired. Penny blinked, relieved to see Amelia had lifted her aim for a warning shot.

The hand loosened, and Penny jerked away, crying out as a hank of hair was torn from her scalp. She stumbled away as Amelia took another shot, this one aimed at the creature that had attacked her.

Penny spun in time to see it lurch for her again, its looming form draped head to toe in dirty, bloodstained bandages. "That's disgusting!" She darted away a moment too late.

The creature wrenched back on her shirt, pulling her back toward it. Penny leaned into the momentum, shoving herself back toward the beast and slamming an elbow into its chest. She felt the crack of dry, snapping bones, but the cottony arms that wrapped around her head showed no hint of pain from the injury.

Penny struggled, slamming her bound fists into the creature's thigh over and over again. It squeezed tighter, smothering her mouth and nose with rancid fabric and filling her lungs with an acidic burn. Penny punched again, driving her knuckles into the same spot. This time, she was rewarded with a hollow snap. The creature's grip faltered and she wriggled free.

Bang. Bang. Bang.

It lurched back as each shot impacted. Blood blossomed on the stained linen bindings, but slowly, dark stains that oozed rather than gushed.

It took a step toward Amelia. Then another. Amelia edged back and let off another round.

"It's not working!" she called.

Two more steps. Corey saw his chance. With a yelp, he scurried behind the bandaged attacker and took off running.

"Coward!" Cisco yelled. He grabbed the fallen branch and held it like a baseball bat, giving it a quick swing for good measure.

The monster snarled and turned to the gorge. It took a few steps after Corey, turning back when a solid *thunk* slammed into its back.

"Look, I know I called him a pussy. Doesn't mean I want him dead. Let's keep the odds at three to one. Okay, asshole?" Penny looked around, eyes desperately seeking some kind of weapon.

That bastard Tobias couldn't even leave us the flamethrower? He'd stripped them of weapons before he left but only missed Amelia's gun. Penny spied a rock and grabbed it, hefting it in her hand, ready to throw.

Amelia pulled the trigger one more time. Instead of a loud bang, it clicked. "Empty!" she yelled, tucking it into the holster to free her hands.

The bandaged monster let out a growl, then pounced, only to hit the ground.

"Boots, you legend!" Penny yelled. The serpent had tangled herself around the creature's feet, tripping it as it attacked.

She lifted her rock and slammed it down on the covered head. Brittle skull crumbled under her hands, and the bandaged monstrosity fell still.

Penny looked up at Cisco. "If you drop that branch on my head, I'll kick your ass."

"Just making sure it's dead." He let it fall to one side after a few moments. "He is dead, right?"

Penny kicked the still form. "I guess so. I'd feel better if it was dismembered or burned. Or both."

Amelia tugged on the ropes binding Penny's wrists, prying one of the knots loose. "We can't do either, and Tobias has Red."

Penny's ropes fell away. She rubbed her wrists and glanced at their escape route. She couldn't see more than a few feet. "I don't think Red's the one we need to worry about."

Amelia groaned. "That's just what I *am* worried about. What if he kills Tobias? I don't think werewolfism is a defense for manslaughter. Is wolfing-out classed as reasonable force?"

Penny's stomach dropped. "Shit. Let's go."

CHAPTER TWENTY

Boots led the way, her soft hiss guiding them through the narrow gorge and through a narrow gap they had missed the first time they had passed it.

Their only light was a tiny flashlight that had been clipped to Cisco's belt, left by Tobias when he'd judged it useless enough to be safe.

Penny squeezed Cisco's hand as he helped her through the gap, then she led Amelia through as she followed.

Amelia squinted into the shadows. "You sure you know where we're going, Boots?"

Boots gave a bored hiss, picking up her pace as the trail opened up again. They passed a straggly bush, then another. When they came to a dead tree, Boots stopped. She tipped her head up and coughed.

Cisco shined the flashlight up. "Is that your ass I can see, Corey?"

Their would-be captor whimpered. "Did you kill it?"

"Yes." Cisco gestured for Corey to climb down. "Get out of the tree, asshole. Hurry up, we have places to be."

Corey began his climb down. A broken branch snapped under his foot and he fell, landing on his back with a thud.

"Fuck," he gasped. Winded, he rolled to his feet, hands up defensively. "I didn't mean that stuff I said back there. Really. I wasn't going to let you die."

"Save the bullshit." Penny motioned toward Boots. "One wrong move and she'll eat your face off. Now, where's Red?"

Corey's face twisted in a jumble of emotions before he finally pointed. "That way. There's a little shack up there, just behind the tree line."

"Don't point. Walk." Cisco jabbed Corey in the back with his stick.

Corey flinched. "Seriously?"

"I'm not leaving you out here to change your mind and come after us, idiot." Cisco poked him again, and Corey set off.

The shack was, as promised, not far off. It sat surrounded by trees, gently lit by the rising moon in a small, overgrown clearing.

Penny pressed herself behind a tree, watching. It was quiet, dark inside.

"What a shame, it looks like no one's home. Can we go now?" Corey eyed the serpent that had him pinned up against his own tree.

Boots had her mouth open, her eyes lazily searching him as if looking for a good place to snack.

"Shh." Wishing she had more than an oversized pebble as a weapon, Penny darted forward to slip beneath a window with Amelia scurrying behind her. Penny rose her head long enough to peek inside. "It's too dark, I can't see anything."

"Cisco?" Amelia called in a loud whisper. "Flashlight!"

The little flashlight flicked toward them, and Penny caught it one-handed. Taking a deep breath, she clicked it on, hiding the light in her palm. Then, she flashed it through the window. "Oh...*hell*."

The narrow beam showed just enough to make her stomach flip. Blood. Blood everywhere.

"Red?" Amelia's eyes were wide, her face pale.

Cisco kicked the door open, his branch held high. He dropped it when he saw the empty room. "What the hell happened here?"

Penny followed him in, stepping carefully to avoid coating her boots in the mess. "What's that?" She pointed into the corner, where a tiny table was covered in melted candles and surrounded by symbols scratched into the old wooden floor. "Tobias really loves his altars, doesn't he?"

"Why wouldn't he?" Penny spun around to see Corey at the door, Boots dangling from a raised fist, gun pointed at her head. "They've brought us so many useful friends."

"Again?" Penny resisted the urge to roll her eyes.

"Where's Red?" Amelia spat. She groped at the small of her back, eyes widening when she came up empty.

"Looking for this?" Corey waggled his gun hand. "You didn't exactly make it hard to steal. You're as dumb as your idiot boyfriend."

Amelia's hands clenched. "I swear to God, if he's hurt, I'll do worse to you. Tell me where he is!"

Corey shrugged. "I really did think they'd be here. Toby

isn't stupid enough to let someone sneak up on him. I figured he'd help me kill you all."

"Asshole." Penny's eyes were locked on Boots. "Let her go."

"I'll let her go, all right. After I blow her brains out." Corey clicked the safety off but paused when he looked at the floor of the cabin. "Outside. I don't wanna mess up one of Toby's spells."

He took three steps back, then grinned, his teeth flashing white in the beam of Cisco's flashlight.

Amelia started forward, and Corey waved the gun toward her. "It's out of bullets, dipshit. Now let Boots go!"

Corey pointed the gun upward and squeezed the trigger. *Bang.*

Amelia screamed.

Corey laughed. "I was packing a spare clip. You didn't even search me properly! God, you're all so stupid, you—"

Whomp.

Corey vanished in a mass of muscle and fur.

Amelia screamed.

Penny threw herself forward as the wolf bounded away. Boots untangled herself and twisted through the grass, trying to wipe the blood off her scales.

Blood? Penny turned.

Corey stared up at the full moon, his eyes glassy. Blood smeared one cheek, and below that was a jagged hole where his throat should have been.

"Penny!" Cisco stumbled over to Penny, supporting Amelia in his arms. "She's been shot."

Amelia struggled out of his grip. "No shit, Cisco." Blood pulsed down her arm, oozing between her fingers as she gripped her bicep. "I'm not the one who's dead, though. It's a good thing Corey can't even hit a target point-blank."

Remembering that Corey had hit her with a paint bullet at close range that time in training, Penny thanked whatever summoned gods might be looking over them at that moment. "You sure you're okay?"

Amelia nodded. "I'm out of the fight, but I can keep up. We have to go after Red!"

"He's gone." Penny frowned at Amelia's raised eyebrow and skeptical glance. "Isn't he?"

"He's behind you." Cisco's voice was awed.

Penny turned slowly, easily spotting the wolf staring back at her from among the trees.

His eyes glittered green in the moonlight, and his fur was red even in the muted colors of the night.

Arooo-oooo. The werewolf—*Red*—howled and bounded off into the trees, stopping just before he vanished into the forest.

"Well? Come on!" Amelia pushed past Cisco and stumbled after him.

Penny quickly caught up to her friend and looped Amelia's good arm over her shoulders. "Cisco, get the gun!"

The wolf led them on a chase through the woods, stumbling downhill through the trees before vanishing as they emerged onto the road.

"Red?" Amelia called. Her voice was weak, and she stumbled as they reached the paved road. "Penny? I don't feel so good."

"It's okay," Penny reassured her. "I see lights up ahead."

Praying it wasn't Tobias, Penny gripped Amelia around

the waist and turned toward the twin glow of headlights moving toward them.

Thank God. Giddy relief flowed through Penny as the dim shape of the car solidified into a familiar Cadillac. *It's over.*

"Crenel!" Penny waved at the agent as he pulled up beside them. "Amelia's hurt."

The agent threw the door open. "Put her in the back. Hurry, there's something out here."

"It's just Red," Penny said, helping Amelia into the back seat. "It's okay, he's helping us."

Crenel gave her an odd look. "This wasn't your friend. Whatever it is, it's not out to help us."

Penny's blood ran cold. "What did it look like?"

Crenel ducked his head up, glancing around worriedly. "Cisco! Get in the car!"

Cisco headed toward them as Crenel moved to the trunk and popped it open.

"Crenel!" Penny snapped. "What did it *look* like?"

Still glancing nervously over his shoulder, Crenel suddenly froze. "Like that." He raised a hand and pointed into the trees by the road.

The bandaged man stood at the side of the road, head misshapen from the blow Penny had inflicted with the rock.

Penny eyed the evil Myther with dismay. *You're at your most vulnerable when you think you've won.* "Glass, you motherfucker. Hate it when you're right."

Crenel snorted. "You've been ignoring your lessons again?" He passed Penny a gun.

"Apparently," she said, taking the weapon from him.

"Stay here. I've got this." Crenel strode forward with a long spear in his hand.

It's not going to work. The thought reached Penny's consciousness just as the creature launched itself into Crenel.

The agent thrust the spear forward, ramming it right through the enemy and out the other side.

The bandaged man didn't even flinch. It grabbed Crenel's arm and twisted it. The agent screamed, and Penny cried out in alarm when a bone popped out, piercing his sleeve.

"Let him go!" Cisco slammed into the creature and knocked it down, then ran into the road to lure the beast away.

Penny grabbed Crenel's shoulder. "Get in the car," she snapped.

He grunted in pain, but obeyed, sliding into the car and collapsing next to Amelia.

Penny kept one eye on Cisco, who dodged back and forth, avoiding the bandaged man's attacks in the middle of the road.

"Cisco!" She waited until his head tipped up slightly in response. "Zombie in the rafters!"

A grin spread over his face as he ducked under another swing of his opponent's arm.

Penny climbed into the idling Cadillac and slammed the door closed. She shoved the clutch in and threw it into gear. The wheels screamed, and the car responded. "Buckle up!"

The Cadillac was as old as the agent who drove it, and it

was just as reliable. The car lurched forward, engine roaring.

Penny nudged the wheel, pressed the accelerator harder, and held her breath as it sped toward the duo fighting in the road.

Cisco slammed what was left of the stick into the bandaged man's face.

"Move, Cisco!" Penny slammed the horn, and right at the last moment, Cisco sprung away.

The car jolted as it rammed the monster. Penny's head smacked against the roof as she drove over its body.

She braked and put the car in park, then hopped out. The trunk was still open, the contents a jumbled mess.

Penny rummaged until she found what she was looking for and walked over to Cisco.

She stood over the pile of linens and admired the tire tracks running over the lumpy mess.

"What now?" Cisco asked.

Penny handed him a machete and shook the lighter in her other hand. "You cut. I'll burn."

CHAPTER TWENTY-ONE

The first fingers of dawn crept over the mountain. Penny's ears still rang from the pummeling beat of the chopper that had airlifted Agent Crenel to the hospital and taken the seared, dismembered body of the bandaged man with it.

"You should have gone," Penny said for the third time.

"Not until I see him," Amelia said. She inspected the fresh bandage on her arm. "It's not bleeding anymore. They did a good job of patching me up, and I can fix the rest when we get back to the Academy."

"You're tougher than I am," Cisco admitted. "I would have gone for the good painkillers and a nice, comfy ride to hospital if it was me."

"It nearly *was* you," Penny reminded him. "You really left it until the last moment to get out of my way, didn't you?"

Cisco shrugged. "I didn't want him to see what you were doing." He hesitated. "Do you think he's really dead this time?"

"If he's not, it's not our problem." Penny's eyes traced the line of the mountains. "But yeah. I think we got him."

A rustle nearby made her sit up. "What was that?"

"It was Boots." Amelia jutted her chin in the direction of the snake, who was headed toward the trees, dragging a pair of jeans. "Uhh, Boots? Where did you get those?"

Boots coughed and continued on her way. Penny shaded her eyes and looked toward the trees. A moment later, she clapped her hands over her eyes. "*Argh!* I'm blinded!"

"Well, you shouldn't have been looking! It's not *my* fault you're between a man and his pants."

"Red!" Amelia jumped to her feet and threw herself at him, yelping when he squeezed her arm by accident.

Penny peeked through her fingers and dropped her hands in relief when she saw Red's jeans were now firmly on his body.

"Ah, sorry, love. Are you all right?" Red carefully placed his arms around her and pulled her to his chest.

"We're fine." Amelia's voice was choked, and when he let her go, her eyes were red. She slapped his chest. "No thanks to you, idiot."

He gave a chagrined smile. "That's true. I'm so sorry, Amelia. I shouldn't have left like that."

"Did you find a cure?" Cisco asked.

Red shook his head. "No. I was so sure! The answer to your question is at the beginning of the journey, it said."

"Are you sure it was real?" Penny asked gently.

"One hundred percent certain," Red said. He dug in a back pocket and pulled a tiny scrap of paper out.

Amelia examined it closely, lips moving as she read the

fortune. She flipped it over to check the back. This time, her slap was hard enough to elicit a grunt. "You moron! This isn't real!"

Red leaned forward to look. "What? How do you know?"

"Real Chinese fortune cookies aren't 'made and packaged in Taiwan,' you numbskull." Amelia screwed the paper up and tossed it on the ground. "All this, and you didn't even find a cure!"

Red blushed. "Aye. But maybe I did get something out of it." At Amelia's quizzical glance, he continued. "I was in full control last night. I was strong and fast, and I saved you all!" He dodged another slap. "Okay, I know you wouldn't have *needed* saving if I wasn't a giant rock-brained idiot, but being a werewolf isn't the end of the world."

"It's the end of my food budget," Amelia muttered. Still, she leaned in and squeezed him tight.

"What happened to you, anyway?" Penny asked. "Do you know where Tobias is?"

Red shook his head. "What a mess it all was. Tobias and Corey found me searching for that altar. I got a bit lost, you see. They tied me up, and Corey figured out pretty quick that I wouldn't be alone out here, that you'd be looking for me."

"So they set a trap for us." Cisco shoved his hands in his pockets. "Did they know you'd wolf out?"

Red grinned, baring his teeth in a decidedly wolfish manner. "Nope. Tobias damn near shit his pants when I started to turn. He ran like a pussy. I started chasing him, but I turned back to look for you lot."

"So, if he didn't know you were infected, does that

mean he didn't summon the first wolf?" Penny frowned, trying to put it together.

Red shook his head. "I don't think he knew anything about it. The bandaged bastard, though? That was all Tobias. Some local legend he dug up. Said once he had a few more sacrifices, he'd be able to control it."

"Where'd you go, anyway?" Amelia pulled back. "You left us to fight that thing alone!"

"Moonset," Red said with a shrug. "I was starting to turn back and I didn't want poor Penny to get an eyeful of me giant dog balls, so I ran. Only I got turned about, and couldn't find my way back."

"Thank you," Penny said gratefully. "Your human balls were horrifying enough. I'm very, *very* glad I didn't see the wolf version."

"Ah, you don't know what you're missing!" Red glanced at Amelia and was crestfallen to see her unimpressed glare.

Penny walked over and wrapped her arms around the couple, squeezing them both tightly. "I'm just glad we're all okay."

Munder sipped at his milk thoughtfully. "You went into the dark wood to find the one you call friend?" The Myther made a sound of curiosity when Penny nodded. "That was very brave. I do not think I could have done that."

"I'm sure you could," Penny said reassuringly. "If you had to save someone you cared about."

"Perhaps." Munder nibbled a cookie. "But I do think you are all very courageous."

"Damn right, we are!" Red raised a mug of beer and toasted the monster. "Aren't we?"

"Some of us are." Amelia ignored his shock and sipped at her pina colada. "Did you go to see Crenel today?"

Penny looked up at the question and nodded. "He's doing well. The arm is almost better, at any rate. He's pissed at the bureau, though. Said he gave them an ultimatum."

"A what now?" Cisco leaned in, his curiosity piqued.

Penny nodded. "He told them they had to commit to faster response times or he and March wouldn't let us go out in the field."

"What?" Cisco's screech brought more than one Myther's attention to him in the bar. "He can't do that!"

"Well, he probably can," Penny admitted. "But I don't think he will. Hopefully, we won't have to find out. Delouise came in as I was leaving, and she said it looks like they'll agree to it."

Cisco slumped back into his chair, relieved. "So, what now?"

Penny grinned, eyes twinkling. "Now, we revel in the fact that we don't have to do our surveillance assignment, or our defense practical, or our defensive driving exam. We got enough credits to pass us for those classes!"

To her surprise, Cisco pouted. "Damn. Do you think Mack will let us take the Jeeps out anyway?"

Penny snorted. "You think he'll say no after we brought those donors in?"

Professor Madera had told Cisco, who of course had told Penny immediately, that the news coverage of the events at Cannon Beach had pulled some very wealthy individuals out of the woodwork, all promising financial support for the college.

Although they were an official training school for the FBI, that funding was going to be used for the private arm of the college March and Blaisey maintained for research purposes.

"Fair call." Cisco brightened. "Anyway, Mack would never say no to you. You're the teacher's pet!"

Penny rolled her eyes and put down her drink. "That's bullshit. You're the one he offered to take skydiving next week."

Smirking, Cisco nodded proudly. "To celebrate passing my first year at the Academy."

Penny smiled too, but wistfully. She swirled her almost-empty drink, watching the bubbles circle the bottom of the glass. "One more semester down. Do you realize that means we're halfway done?"

Cisco's face softened. "Halfway. Just one year to go."

Penny brightened and raised her glass. She gave a short whistle toward a nearby table, and Bacchus looked up from his conversation with an undersized bunyip.

The glass filled, and Penny held it out toward her friends. "To one more year of ass-kicking fun. Together."

"Together!" Glasses clinked as Cisco, Amelia, and Red echoed Penny's toast.

"Together." Munder smiled, quietly tapping his glass against Penny's. "And to friends."

THE END

Book three in the series, Pixels and Poltergeists, is coming soon and will available at Amazon and through Kindle Unlimited.

Since myth and legend started coming to life, Penny has seen everything. Werewolves, ghosts, witches, gods, spooky video games... wait, what?

It seems the stories told through the ages aren't all as old as the hills (or Agent Crenel). Weird stuff is coming through, the sort of stuff only recent generations could have come up with.

It's not just Nigerian princes and 'like for a cure' memes, either. One of Penny's friends stumbled on a conspiracy involving a secret government agency, some missing people… and a computer game.

Now, he's missing, and it's up to her to find him.

Penny and Boots are working the case with Cisco, while trying to dodge creepy professors, dealing with break ins, and recovering from the Worst. Date. Ever. (It wasn't her fault, really!).

What do you get when you cross Area 51, Space Invaders, and a rip in the Veil? One BIG mystery. And Penny and Boots will solve it… if they don't die first.

AUTHOR NOTES - AMY HOPKINS

OCTOBER 19, 2019

If you're reading this, it's been at least a month since Snakes and Shadows came out. Here in Australian time... it's still six days until launch. Well, a week in US time, because I'm ahead of them but behind you. Clear as mud?

Did you like it? I mean, I guess you didn't *hate* it if you're here. You liked it enough to grab book two. Is it selling well? I always get nervous before an LMBPN launch. When I launched my own series, it was just my own time and money on the line. Now? There are so many people invested in the success of every book.

Here's where I hope to be when this little letter of mine goes live: It'll be November, so I'll be in Christmas prep mode. Hopefully by then (like, SERIOUSLY), my dog will know that poo is for outside, not in my damn hallway. I won't lie — I know I won't have started my Christmas shopping yet. I'm notorious for doing all that at the last minute.

I'd like to be really close to getting my yellow belt in Tae Kwon-Do. I'm getting my yellow stripe on Tuesday, so it'll be a stretch, but I'm practicing really hard and have the advantage of ten months observing classes before I joined. Also, I'd like my blister to be healing. Ouch-face-emoji.

Most of all, I'd love, love, LOVE to see a little orange flag on my books. I want people to be buying, reading, loving them. I want people to count Penny and Boots as a couple of new friends, not just words on a page. To walk the streets of Portland beside me, not just read it in a book.

So... how did I do? I'll probably have forgotten this whole thing in a month. Remind me. Tell me if I met my goals (and I'll tell you if my blisters healed)!

- A. H.
P.S. I'm still salty about Diego.

AUTHOR NOTES - MICHAEL ANDERLE

NOVEMBER 21, 2019

Thank you for reading this story and making it to the back for our *Author Notes!*

Sometimes... No, scratch that. ALL THE DAMNED TIME, you can't be sure what will come out of Amy's mouth or be typed by Amy's little fingers. One of the things I find so fun about her is her funny unpredictability.

She is like a little Australian (Tasmanian) Devil, with a chunk of attitude on one shoulder and a heart of gold three sizes larger on the other.

If you have a few minutes and care to drop Amy a note, just open the reviews and leave her a message. You and I both know that for her, they will be little Christmas gifts received a bit early, or late, or really, *really* early for NEXT year.

Right now, we are in the last third of the month—20th-30th (we are on the 21st at the moment.) I know Amy is sitting on the 22nd. I've been to Australia which is one (1) hour behind the new day. I'm pretty sure it's sometime around 2:30 in the morning for her.

Which is FRIDAY! (WOOT)

I am traveling between Las Vegas and Los Angeles at the moment. Above me are masses of clouds arrayed like warships ready to pass through the sky over the mountains as we travel south by southwest. In the distance, shadows play against the land that is jutting into the sky, and it looks *fantabulous*.

However, the sun is aimed right at my stomach, streaming through the front windshield, and I'm burning up.

I'll reach LA and be nothing but a burnt skeleton…yuk.

Why does my imagination always go for the dark side?

Well, lunch was too much food, and I'm in a losing battle with my eyelids. I wish you well in whatever you are doing at the moment. May the day bring you something special and cool like you reading this book has brought me.

Ad Aeternitatem,

Michael

CONNECT WITH THE AUTHORS

Amy Hopkins Social
Website:
https://amyhopkinsauthor.com
Facebook:
https://www.facebook.com/thespellscribe

Michael Anderle Social
Website:
http://www.lmbpn.com

Email List:
http://lmbpn.com/email/

Facebook Here:
www.facebook.com/TheKurtherianGambitBooks/